A FAIR IN TIME

Adventures in the Turkey Capital of the World

Dave McCauley

The events described in <u>Early Adventures</u> are told as accurately as I can remember them. The short stories in <u>Too Good to be True</u>, are complete fiction. The characters, names, incidents and plots in those stories are products of the author's imagination or are used fictitiously. To add context to those stories, some real individuals from the period are mentioned.

ISBN 978-1-64440-348-8

To all whose names I remembered and all those whose names I've forgotten.

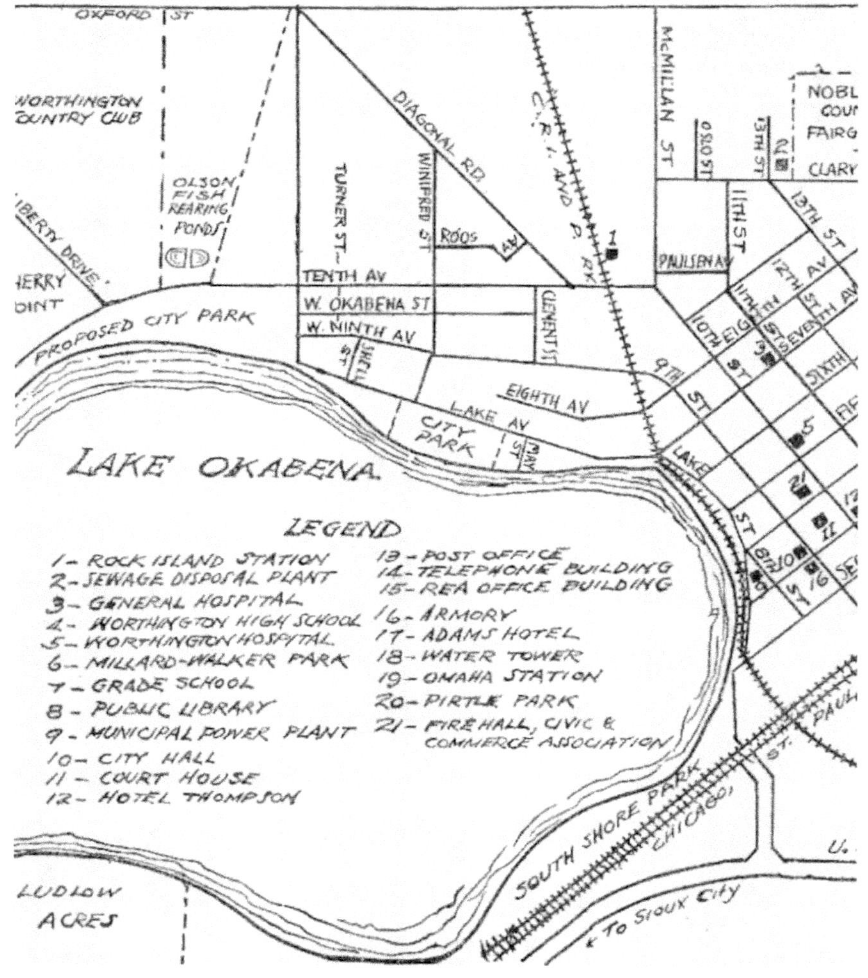

TO SIOUX FALLS
U.S. 16
OXFORD ST
WORTHINGTON COUNTRY CLUB
McMILLAN ST
NOBLES COUNTY FAIRG
CLARY
OLSON FISH REARING PONDS
OLSON ST
13TH ST
LIBERTY DRIVE
TURNER ST
WINIFRED ST
DIAGONAL RD
C.R.I. AND P. RY.
11TH ST
13TH ST
CHERRY POINT
ROOS AV
PAULSEN AV
12TH AV
7TH ST
11TH ST
TENTH AV
CLEMENT ST
10TH ST
EIGHT
SEVENTH AV
PROPOSED CITY PARK
W. OKABENA ST
W. NINTH AV
9TH ST
SIXTH
SHELL ST
EIGHTH AV
LAKE AV
CITY PARK
MAY ST
LAKE OKABENA
LAKE ST
6TH ST
SOUTH SHORE PARK
CHICAGO ST.
ST. PAUL
U.
LUDLOW ACRES
TO SIOUX CITY
LEGEND
1 - ROCK ISLAND STATION
2 - SEWAGE DISPOSAL PLANT
3 - GENERAL HOSPITAL
4 - WORTHINGTON HIGH SCHOOL
5 - WORTHINGTON HOSPITAL
6 - MILLARD-WALKER PARK
7 - GRADE SCHOOL
8 - PUBLIC LIBRARY
9 - MUNICIPAL POWER PLANT
10 - CITY HALL
11 - COURT HOUSE
12 - HOTEL THOMPSON
13 - POST OFFICE
14 - TELEPHONE BUILDING
15 - REA OFFICE BUILDING
16 - ARMORY
17 - ADAMS HOTEL
18 - WATER TOWER
19 - OMAHA STATION
20 - PIRTLE PARK
21 - FIRE HALL, CIVIC & COMMERCE ASSOCIATION

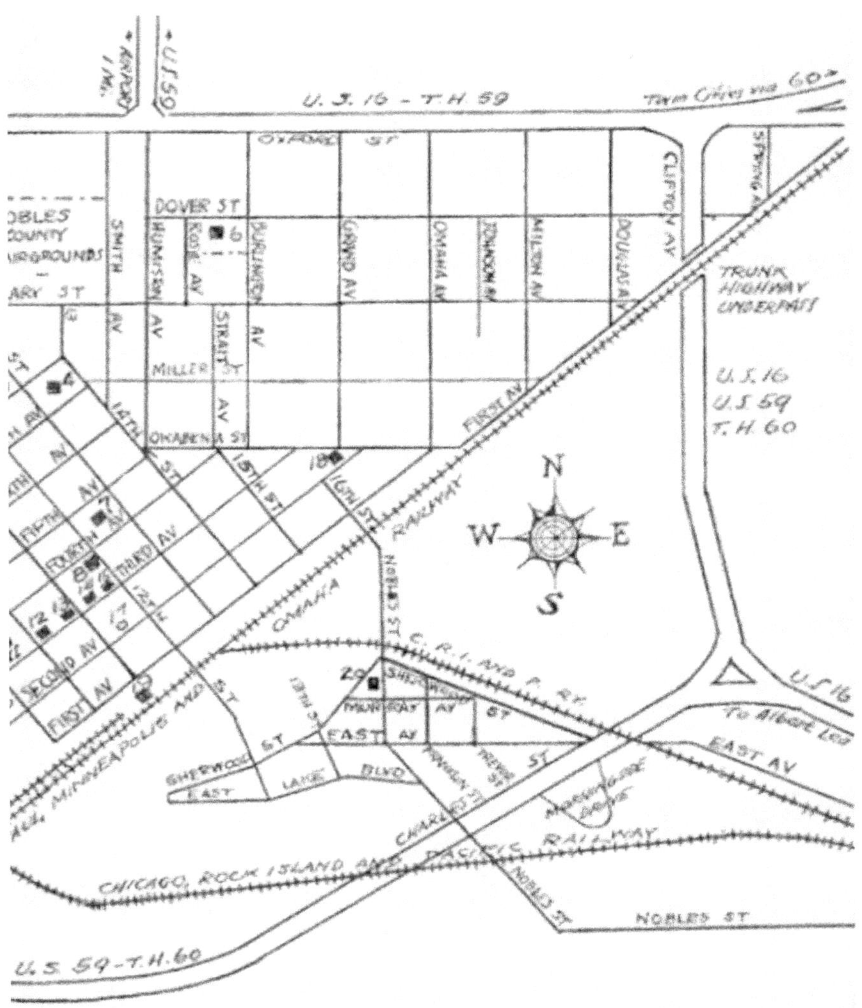

CITY MAP OF WORTHINGTON, MINNESOTA
Circa 1950

TABLE OF CONTENTS

FORWARD

Interstate Highway 90 begins in Boston, Massachusetts, and stretches westward across the northern United States ending up in Seattle, Washington, slightly over three thousand miles from the Atlantic to Pacific. Driving toward Seattle from Boston you reach the exact midpoint of your journey at Worthington, Minnesota, on the eastern edge of the Coteau des Prairies – highland of the prairies; you are about forty miles east of the South Dakota border. The countryside around Worthington is gently rolling; mostly farm fields covered with corn and soy beans. Its higher elevation means strong winds so you see tall wind generators scattered across the fields; their long blades twirling majestically. Worthington is a bustling city with a population of over 12,000 people. It's a commercial center with a large pork processing plant, a regional hospital, a community college and a couple of large industrial plants. At modern freeway speeds you'll bypass Worthington in just a few minutes but if you look to the south as you pass, you may spot the "Pioneer Village," a collection of buildings and artifacts preserving the Worthington of the past. Like the Pioneer Village, this book gives you a chance to look back at the city as it was when I was a youngster living there.

If you travel back in time to 1939, you'll be driving through Worthington on US Highway 16, the precursor to Interstate 90. Instead of buy-passing the city, Highway 16 leads you right down 10th Street, the main thoroughfare.

There were no motels in 1939 but you could get a room right downtown at the big and beautiful Thompson Hotel or at one of the cabin courts along the highway.

I was one year old in 1939 when my family arrived in Worthington. There were four of us then, Steve and Lillian, my mother and father and Kerry, my older brother. My father, a professional musician, had joined the "Tiny Little Orchestra," as their lead trumpeter.

Worthington is built around the east shore of Lake Okabena, a potato-shaped lake about 2 miles long and a mile across. When we arrived, two railroads, the Rock Island, and the Chicago and Northwestern ran through town. Highway 16, a major east-west US highway then, and highways 60 and 59 all passed right down Tenth Street, the city's main thoroughfare.

By 1939, the agony of the depression waned and Worthington was a hubbub of new economic activity. The local merchants, seeking to capitalize on their new found economic prosperity led by a growing turkey industry proudly declared Worthington "The Turkey Capitol of the World" and inaugurated a "King Turkey Day" celebration complete with a street carnival and big parade. A whirlwind of change had begun; led by a phalanx of active boosters determined to see the city thrive and grow. They set out to improve everything and they largely succeeded.

When we left Worthington for a short stint in Mason City, Iowa in 1948, trains were pulled by steam locomotives, everyone used ice boxes, farmers still used horses, many backyards had outdoor toilets, you could rent rowboats at the Cherry Point Store, and there was a fish pond in front of Fenstermacher's Mobil Station on Tenth Street. When we moved back to Worthington one year later all of those things were gone. There were new and exciting sights and sounds to be sure but nothing could replace the wonderment of those earlier times. Anyway, rummaging through the cluttered attic of my memories is a delight and I am pleased to find so many treasures still largely intact and, in most cases, still interesting enough to recount.

This book is divided into two parts, Early Adventures and Stories Too Good to Be True. The Early Adventures are as accurate as I can recount them but memory does play tricks and, unfortunately, most of the places and people I describe have vanished long ago so you'll have to imagine them as I describe them. Stories Too Good To Be True are all fiction but people as old as I am may recognize names here and there as I've sometimes included real people where ever I could just for the delight of bringing them back to life. Everyone, it seems, has vivid early childhood memories and I'm no exception.

Join me in stories that follow as we wander through Worthington from 1940 to 1959.

EARLY ADVENTURES

The stories and essays that follow recount my memories of Worthington as I grew up. Hope you will enjoy revisiting Worthington with me.

A Grand Tour

My Father was a musician, he played trumpet in the Tiny Little Orchestra, a job which took him away from home most nights. While we missed having him with us in the evening, there were a couple of benefits to his absence. My mother liked to read and many nights my brother and I would get bundled into the big bed, on either side of Mom, and she would read to us until her eyes threatened to fall out. The other benefit was we often were allowed to accompany Dad as he went downtown to pay bills at the end of the month, usually on a Saturday morning.

It wasn't until after World War II that we got a car, so trips downtown when I was small were made on foot. The custom then was for most people to pay bills in person, and on Saturday there was usually a line at the more popular stops - the Telephone Company, the Gas Company, and City Hall. We made all those and more - I guess we had a charge account at Montgomery

Wards and later a home mortgage at the Savings and Loan. Paying in person meant meeting and talking with many of the people in town we knew, and I enjoyed the attention we got as Dad took us from place to place. I suppose Mom, in turn, enjoyed the peace and quiet she had when we weren't underfoot.

The upstairs apartment that we lived in wasn't that far from the center of town, but trips downtown, on foot, were not wasted and we often did more than just pay bills. If our hair was long we would be ushered into Pop Smith's Barbershop (next door to the "Corn Crib" or Schafer's Market, I'm not sure which) to wait our turn and absorb the unique atmosphere that only a barbershop has - watching Tenth Street pass in review in front of the big window and listening to "manly" conversation. Then it would be our turn and Pop would put the booster seat board over the arms of the barber's chair; we would clamber up to be swathed in a cape and a paper collar wrapped around our neck protecting us from hair clippings. A few deft snips with the scissors, some close work with the clippers and then dollop of hot lather around our ears and neck. I'll admit that the sinister sound of the straight-edge razor being stropped took the fun out of that last traditional ending to the haircut - having your neck shaved. A splash of "Lucky Tiger" hair tonic, a generous dusting of talcum powder with that long soft brush, and we were on our way.

Down the street from the barbershop, Rickbeil's Hardware was an exciting stop on those Saturday jaunts. Aisles full of interesting and unusual tools, hinges, bolts, cap screws, paint, putty, ladders, shovels, sandpaper and guns. Just below the high pressed tin ceiling the walls were adorned with mounted hunting trophies, dominated by a moose head at one end and a caribou head at the other - or maybe it was a bear head. It was long ago and I was pretty small. The only rival to Rickbeil's mounted menagerie was the collection at Meier Brothers' Pool Hall across the street. Meier's went in for exotic fare - an albino pheasant for example. I'm not sure which taxidermy zoo was considered tops but I do remember the day Meier Brothers' put the stuffed two-headed calf in their window - the Rickbeil's Hardware collection fell forever into second place.

The two-headed calf sent a wave of excitement through town. Tenth Street was always busy on Saturday, but this was something! People packed the sidewalk and crowded into the street and the newspaper had headlines (I'm a little fuzzy on that but you could look it up). Dad was never much of a beer drinker so I didn't have the opportunity to observe the crowd inside the Pool Hall but it must have been just as exciting inside as it was out. Perhaps if you worked your way past the bar and into the pool room things would have been somewhat calmer.

Stuffed animals, loud talk, laughter, music, and excitement may have been the norm in the barroom, but in the pool room, tranquility reigned. Dim light reflected from the green felt covered tables and the soft snick of colliding ivory balls shut out all the two-headed hubbub going on in the front.

The few times I was allowed in the pool room as a small boy were exciting indeed. I clearly remember my first time in the balcony at church, my first close-up look at an airplane, my first ride on a Ferris wheel and my first visit to Meier's pool room; all four evoked the same sense of wonderment. Maybe it's the orderly nature of pool rooms - tables arranged just so, high seated chairs with foot rests lining the dark paneled walls, the islands of light in the smoky twilight. Maybe it's the silent ballet of the players as they glide along the tables, waving their cues like magic wands and then, with exaggerated deliberation, stroking them - all under the vigilant and silent gaze of the audience seated along the wall in those high chairs like so many Muses in their gloomy shrines. There were no stuffed animals in the pool room. I'd bet that the pool players didn't know about that two-headed calf out front and probably didn't care either.

During the summer we'd turn right and head down Second Avenue toward the lake and, if we'd been well-behaved, stop at the Worthmore Creamery walk-up window for an ice cream cone (Campbell Soup replaced Worthmore and then Campbell Soup vanished). When I got older, we'd go into the Worthmore Ice Cream Parlor and enjoy sundaes and malts. One of their deadly delights was a super-banana split called the "Pigs Dinner." It was served in a wooden trough – three scoops of different flavored ice cream on the banana, marshmallow crème, nuts, maraschino cherries, chocolate syrup and whipped cream.

By now noon would be upon us, announced by the whistle at the power plant. What a magnificent and imposing structure the power plant was, with its tall graceful smokestack towering over the city like the spire of a great gothic cathedral. In fact the power plant building itself was somewhat cathedral like - a silent and imposing Art Deco exterior with high windows. Inside there were gleaming floors and polished dynamos humming steadily, all tended by a few engineers who appeared and disappeared noiselessly while performing the unknown priestly rituals of their craft. On a school field trip we toured the plant and were taken back into the inner sanctum - the boiler room - and allowed to peep through a hole into the fiery furnace, half expecting to see Shadrach, Meshach and Abed-nego in the flames. Now I know what it must have been like to visit the Oracle at Delphi.

Signs warned us away from the place along the lake shore where the stream vent for the power plant came out - and indeed, much to our delight, sudden geysers often erupted with great white billowing clouds of steam. You knew mighty forces were at work in that place.

I'm sure that by now Dad was ready to head homeward. We'd go north along the lake, walking on the Rock Island Railroad tracks that ran along the shore, then turn east up Fourth Avenue and climb the hill past Martin Chevrolet, the harness shop and fire station.

When we were old enough to go downtown by ourselves we'd go to the harness shop and buy a pair of rawhide shoe laces for a dime, just to watch the harness maker cut them from a large leather hide. The Firestone garage was next and then across Tenth Street; Ahlf's Drug Store, Wick's Jewelry and Dingler's Sporting Goods. Crossing the alley, there was a white frame building that sold second hand furniture. Once we'd reached that point it was just a few blocks to home.

The apartment we lived in then was rented from Hannah Thompson Parker of the Hotel Thompson family. She lived in a dark stucco house on the corner of Sixth Avenue and Twelfth Street. If our rent was due, that would be Dad's last stop. We would wait in the front room while Dad counted out the money. What an interesting and unusual room to wait in - love birds, incense burners, Chinese lamps with fringed shades, rock crystals, a polished abalone shell and other bric-a-brac surrounded us on all sides - it was like being in a museum. I was so fascinated by her possessions that I don't have the slightest memory of Hannah Thompson Parker at all! The Thomson-Parker house still stands and looks today much as it did then!

When we got home we'd rush in to tell Mom everything we did and everyone we saw and everyplace we went. I wonder whatever happened to that two-headed calf.

The Worthington Municipal power plant stopped generating electricity in 1982 and was demolished in 1993. Photo courtesy Nobles County Historical Society.

Dreaming of Steam

Not long ago on a hot day I was sitting in a jetliner at the end of a runway waiting to take off. Because of the heat, the door to the cockpit was left open (this was before 9/11) and I watched as the pilots performed their final pre-flight tasks. As we taxied into position for take-off, the captain removed his flight officer's hat, reached under his seat, fished a worn railroad locomotive engineer's cap out of his flight bag, pulled it on with a flourish, settled back in his seat and put his right hand on the throttles. The cockpit door closed and the jet engines began to roar; for a moment I thought I detected the faint, acrid smell of coal smoke! As the plane accelerated down the runway, I knew that I wasn't the only little boy who dreamed of growing up to be a railroad locomotive engineer someday.

* * *

I was too young to remember it, but when we lived on East Avenue, Mom used put my older brother and me in a baby buggy and walk down to where the Chicago and Northwestern railroad tracks crossed Twelfth Street so we would be entertained by watching the busy switch engine and the freight and passenger trains that came by regularly. The depot and railroad yard were busy and important places then, trains - I mean trains pulled by steam engines - were still the most popular mode of commercial transportation. The Worthington train yard boasted a round house, a huge wooden water tank and a big concrete coaling tower. With a local ice house, freight trains with refrigerated box cars often stopped to take on ice with their coal and water.

To keep passers-by and automobiles safe, there was a little flag shack right next to where the tracks crossed Twelfth Street. Whenever a train approached, the flagman would step out of this shack, walk to the center of the road and wave a red flag to stop traffic. At night he waved a kerosene lantern with a red globe.

The passenger depot still stands at the head of Eleventh Street, built solidly of brick with a slate roof and large canopy covering the passenger loading platform. The area around the building and the passenger loading platform is paved with red brick. Although under one roof, the depot building was divided into separate wings with an open space between. The west wing housed the Depot Cafe and the east held the waiting room, ticket agent's office, baggage claim office and Railway Express office. Today, we think of UPS and FEDEX as our package delivery service, back then it was Railway Express.

Between passenger trains the building was mostly deserted, the occasional clatter of the telegraph in the ticket agent's office and the steady tick of the large clock in the waiting room were about the only signs of life until shortly before a train was due.

When a passenger train was scheduled to arrive, the depot would spring to life; much like the hustle and bustle of today's modern big airports. Travelers queued up at the ticket windows and departing passengers clustered around the baggage check, pushing suitcases, trunks, valises and boxes at the clerk. The wooden benches began to accumulate a variety waiting occupants - everyone talking in hushed, a most furtive, tones as though not to reveal anything personal to the growing crowd of strangers. Tickets and baggage claim checks were issued with much stamping and punching - re-assuring the recipients of their validity and value. Soon the crowd would begin to overflow onto the outdoor platform as the anticipation mounted.

Today it is hard to imagine there was a crowd on Worthington's railroad station platform. Passenger trains then were a tangible, visible contact with the distant world - newspaper and radio were our only other day to day connections - so seeing a train was proof that all the exciting events we only heard about or read about were really taking place. The platform would be full - I mean packed full - of people waiting for the train. Passengers dressed up in coats and hats, families waiting for a son, or father, or mother; soldiers and sailors maybe leaving home forever - everyone talking, hugging or holding hands. You couldn't help becoming more and more excited as the clock ticked toward the arrival time. People craned their necks looking for any tell-tale sign. When the high-wheeled baggage carts, heaped with mail bags and luggage were tugged into position on the platform, everyone began edging closer to the tracks. Stragglers hurried to the ticket windows, the last few occupants of the waiting room began collecting parcels and purses - all eyes were on the tracks.

"There it is!" some sharp-eyed youngster would be the first to yell.

Just a smudge of smoke over the horizon and then the distant moan of the whistle, soon the yellow headlight would appear and each puff of smoke would be clearly visible. Everyone stood still, their gaze riveted on the approaching train, if we moved it might be scared away and or not stop!

This train doesn't even slow down, a fast freight heading west pulling cattle and freight thunders past on a swirl of coal dust and cinders. Mothers held their children tightly, believing that a speeding train could suck people to their death under those steel wheels.

Then, at last, we'd see the real thing, entranced by the sounds of a slowing steam locomotive - sighing puffs of smoke, clanging bell and hissing steam surround the black engine as it rolls and swaggers into the station. The flagman strolls from his little shack along the tracks and waves his red flag to stop traffic as the locomotive followed by several dark green passenger cars, a dining car and railway express baggage car, glides across Twelfth Street into the station, squeaking and shuddering to a halt. Just before the train stops, the conductor opens a passenger car door and with the elegant gracefulness of a ballerina swings lightly to the platform, his silver buttoned black uniform and round cap showing that he is in charge and all present are under his command. At his signal the other car doors open, small step stools are placed below each door by white coated porters and the arriving passengers begin to appear, closely scrutinized by the waiting crowd on the platform.

A Grandmother in a hat of tight felt, net and feathers hesitates at the doorway and then accepts the conductor's steadying hand and steps down lightly onto the platform. Fathers, grandfathers, sons, daughters, wives and uncles grin shyly as they too step down onto the platform into the bright sun. A small boy, his face blank with apprehension, pauses until a shout from a large, overall clad grandfather lights up his face. He jumps over the step-stool and is swept up shoulder high and carried away. As passengers depart, boxes, cartons, crates, mailbags, even (in the spring) baby chicks are quickly unloaded onto carts and pulled away. Next the waiting luggage and mail is swiftly loaded into the baggage car.

The conductor anxiously surveys the platform, waving the newcomers aboard. Unlike the lingering farewells in the movies, people climb quickly into the cars - too slow and you don't get a good seat! Faces appear at the car windows, smiling, mouthing goodbyes and waving silently to their escorts on the platform.

The mighty locomotive broods nervously at the head of the train, wreathed in a clouds of smoke and steam, sounding alive with the heart-beat rhythms of pumps and compressors, the sighing of escaping steam, the muffled rumble of fire deep within and the waves of heat that wash over those who venture near; waiting for the engineer's hand on the throttle. A small boy wanders close and putting his hands on his knees; he squats forward to look under the mighty leviathan as the engineer leans out of the cab window high above and watches.

Raising his hand the Conductor intones the call, "ALLLL ABOARD!" The locomotive bell begins to clang, two deep bellows from the whistle and the engineer eases forward on the throttle. The locomotive pauses momentarily as though drawing a deep breath - then the huge, black spoked driving wheels groan forward. The first, labored explosion of smoke shoots skyward with a mighty roar and then another and another as the train begins to roll forward. The conductor swings aboard the now moving train with the same graceful nonchalance with which he alighted and the train is again underway. A white coated steward with a polished bronze face and hair like a pewter colored helmet flashes a wide departing smile from the doorway of the dining car. Soon the winking red light on back of the last car disappears.

The platform empties as quickly as it filled. The proud grandfather, carrying a large suitcase, leads his grandson to a visit in the country and the traveling man with his valise in one hand and sample case in the other heads toward the Adams Hotel. The hatted grandmother is tugged away by two small boys both talking excitedly; the baggage carts disappear and the waiting room is empty again except for the ticking clock and the clatter of the telegraph.

The Chicago and Northwestern (now the Union Pacific) depot still exists, largely in its original condition. The lovely turret-shaped cupola has been removed but that's the only visible major alteration. Photo courtesy Nobles County Historical Society.

Potato Bug Tea

By the start of World War II we had moved to Twelfth Street, across from where St. Mary's school stands today. Our home was an apartment on the top floor of a small two-story duplex. It wasn't a very imposing place then and eventually it was torn down to make room for a parking lot. The old St. Mary's Church was still standing and Judge Vincent Hollaren's house occupied the St. Mary's grade school's present location. Most of the houses in the neighborhood were old enough to have sheds or barns out back; people no longer had horses or cows in those sheds but many still kept ducks, chickens or pigeons.

Our apartment was heated by a gas stove in the living room and a small kerosene space heater that Mom would put in the bathroom when we took baths. Someone had to go all the way down to the basement to light the water heater when you wanted hot water - then you had to remember to go back down and turn it off before you ended up with steam and a broken water heater! You had to always be alert - the pan under the ice box had to be emptied regularly, the ice man's card with the proper weight showing had to be put in the window at the proper time. Don't forget the milk on the step - it froze in the winter and soured in the summer - each wash load had to be timed - no automatics then, no oven timers - one lapse and there was disaster. We'd never have survived if TV had arrived before household automation.

Our neighborhood had lots of kids our age, making it seem safe, so Mom allowed us to roam pretty freely in spite of the fact I wasn't even in school yet. It worked out. Doug Fiola fell into a cactus patch in his own back yard, I fell off the roof of an entryway in Paulson's back yard into a thorn hedge, and my brother, Kerry stepped on a board and put a nail through his foot - but those events always happened in a crowd so everyone got alerted, nobody broke anything, and there were few trips to the hospital; as I said, it worked out.

Large gardens were common and in summer evenings backyards came alive with hoes, hand cultivators and watering cans.

Mr. Thompson was our favorite gardener; I think he got as big a kick out of us being in his garden as we did. We would help him make "tea" for the potato bugs (I think it was arsenic and water - there were few garden insecticides then), or turn the crank on his grinder while he sharpened his clippers, or fill the sprinkler can for him or bring him tin foil for the ball he was growing in his garage.

This tranquil universe was interrupted by the outbreak of World War II. The war effort was largely beyond our understanding but we'd get involved at times - black out curtains and air-raid drills complete with a visit from the local air-raid warden in his silver World War I helmet. We peeled labels off cans, cut out their bottoms and flatten them for recycling. When I started school in 1943, we bought savings stamps that, when you had enough, could be turned in for war bonds. Mom had ration books for sugar and meat and Dad gave his gas ration coupons to the dance band he played with so they could drive to the towns where the dances were held. My cousin Roger, my uncle Bob and my aunt Marge were all in the war. Dad got his induction notice in 1943 but didn't pass the physical.

The first thing everyone noticed was that many items we took for granted became very hard to find. One morning Mom took us to Hively's neighborhood store to shop for some groceries. Mom fidgeted impatiently as Mr. Hively ignored her and waited on a customer who had arrived after we did. After the customer left, Mom barely held back an angry rebuke before Mr. Hively told her he was sorry for making her wait. He then reached under the counter and brought up a cluster of ripe bananas which he handed to Mom.

"I'm saving these for regular customers and didn't want that stranger to know I had them. We only got a few and with a war on who knows when we'll get any more."

When the dance band went on overnight road trips, dad often passed the time shopping for hard to find items. Once, to Mom's delight he brought home a couple of pairs of nylon stockings, a rare find during the war.

Sometimes the war came closer than we could imagine. One cloudy day in the spring of 1943 a B-17 bomber being ferried to the east coast got lost and missed a refueling stop at Sioux Falls. It spotted Worthington's small air field and somehow managed to land. I was outside when the mighty plane roared over so low that the earth shook and I thought it was going to take the brick chimney right off the top of our house! Lucky for us a friend of ours, a school teacher from Slayton named Audrey James, was visiting and she had a CAR! We all piled into her Model A coupe and headed for the airport. I must have been in the middle, on the bottom, because all I remember about the trip to the airport was the shiny parking brake lever next to the gear shift. When we got to the airfield a large crowd had gathered around the plane; we stood back in AWE!

What a sight - I'd never, ever, seen anything so magnificent, so powerful and so exciting. I can still see that beautiful Flying Fortress towering over me.

Without a car, grocery shopping meant a trip downtown on foot to Anderson's Fairway Market on Tenth Street next to Benson's Furniture store. Wooden floors, canvas awnings, vegetables displayed on flat tables with a fine mist to keep them moist, lugs of peaches, pears, apricots and plums gave the store an exotic air. You were waited on by a battery of clerks who fetched items from the shelves and hauled then to the checkout counter. Butchers sliced, weighed and wrapped to your exact order. It was a good thing that we were waited on in the store as carrying those groceries home was not fun. In the winter Mom would phone in her order to Shafer's Market - they delivered.

My brother, Kerry, is a year older than I am so he went off to school first leaving me home on the step of our porch to watch the parade of neighborhood kids passing our door as they headed up the street to Central Grade School. Not only was I left out, the older boys (probably second graders) loudly announced what they would do to little stay-at-homes if they ever caught one. I soon learned to stay indoors until they were long past. Life must have been dull that year with most of the neighbor kids gone all day because I remember little that I did by myself when Kerry was in school.

Soon it was my turn to walk those five blocks down Twelfth Street into another universe. Hattie Fenske was the principal - of course you must address her as "Miss Fenske" - and her school was a model of decorum and discipline. We soon learned to walk in the halls, in single file, quietly, and with caps off. To this day I whip my cap off as soon as I come indoors - expecting Miss Fenske to appear if I'm the least bit sluggardly. I had no other standard by which to judge our principal, but she always seemed to me to be just what you expect one to look like, sound like and act like. We did get our money's worth from her in the unforgettable lessons of proper conduct and respect for persons with authority.

By the time I advanced to second grade, the school started a "hot lunch" program. Parents volunteered as cooks and lunchroom attendants. We ate in the old gym - a small dark afterthought stuck onto the rear of the school where the "crook" of the two wings old Central grade School came together. The food was simple - soup or stew, buttered bread and little half pint bottle of milk. By the time I was in fourth grade a new gym and cafeteria had been built and regular, government supervised lunches were the norm.

The five years I spent at Central Grade School passed without much excitement. I remember VE Day - we all assembled in front of the school, said the Pledge of Allegiance, sang "America the Beautiful" and "The Star Spangled Banner", and got the rest of the day off!

The only educational triumph I remember was the day I learned to spell "because." I could hardly wait to get home to impress Mom! My grades were good but my only claim to notoriety was an "F" I got in conduct in the third grade. Kenny Moore was able to explain to his parents that his "F" was no big deal because Dave McCauley had gotten the same thing!

My parents were puzzled by my bad behavior. They learned that I was almost totally deaf due to a lingering ear infection. That was only partially true as I was (and still am) prone to making mischief. The infection was treated and my conduct was never graded that low again.

Across the street, facing the front entrance to the school stood the Carnegie Library. My mother enjoyed reading and took us to the library often. We were regulars at their Saturday morning story hour. The children's library was in the basement in a comfortable, book lined room with low tables we could sit around. Potted plants grew on the window sills and in the back was an aquarium filled with aquatic plants, large snails and maybe fish (I don't ever remember seeing any fish in those weeds - just snails). The children's librarian was Mrs. Schar. She was friendly, helpful and kind.

Burdened with a physical disability that required the use of crutches, she moved slowly and seemed to operate at our level which made us like her even more. We were read stories, saw puppet shows and demonstrations, and once we were treated to a set of carved Russian dolls - the kind that nestle one inside the other. Mostly it was reading, but we didn't care what they did, it was fun. After the story hour, Mom would help us pick out books. You could always get an idea of how popular a book was doing by looking at the checkout card. At that time, the borrower's name was written on the card and the date it was checked out stamped next to the name. Remember those little date stamps fastened to the pencil so the clerk could write your name and stamp the date without changing implements? Often our name would appear several times on the same card - I wonder if Mom got tired of reading the same book over and over. At last we would head home loaded with treasures.

The Carnegie library shortly after it was constructed. Demolished and replaced by the Nobles County Memorial Library. Photo courtesy Nobles County Historical Society.

Who was that at the Door?

I was sitting on the front steps one summer evening not long ago, watching the sunset and listening to the sounds of twilight. Slowly the noises of the neighborhood slipped away into the dark shadows until a tranquil stillness enveloped everything. As I sat watching and listening to the end of the day I heard echoes of a long forgotten sound. It could have been wind chimes or maybe a neighbor rattling around a cluttered kitchen, but to me it was a far more enchanting sound, a sound heard long before I knew anything about wind chimes.

Mother heard it first. She went to the cupboard where she kept special things and brought out a pot with a loose handle and an enamel kettle that leaked and a galvanized pail that had a small crack and a teakettle with a hole in the bottom and then she went into the bedroom and came out with her good scissors. I didn't have any idea what she was doing but soon I heard the sound too. It was a faint ringing and clattering; rhythmic and random at the same time; music and noise coming from the same source.

At last Mom said, "It's a tinker. Let's hurry before he goes by."

We gathered the assortment of utensils, went downstairs and out the door, stepping outside just in time. Coming down the street was a mule, shuffling along disinterestedly; head bobbing up and down with each measured stride. The mule was pulling a strange looking wagon with rubber tires, like a car, and a high box with sides that opened revealing racks and shelves. Hanging from the box were every imaginable household and kitchen tool you every saw; pots, pans, kettles, ladles, sieves, colanders, spoons, shredders, peelers, mashers, strainers and carpet beaters. Swinging to the bobbing gait of the mule they rattled and clanked and tinkled with a most inviting sound.

Walking alongside the wagon was a short man clad in baggy black trousers, a grey shirt and dark brown vest. His shoes, once black, had long since lapsed into a dusty, scuffed, run-over grey. On his head was a well-worn fedora hat, sweat stained, dusty and drooping. His wrinkled skin was dark and a black moustache and bushy eyebrows almost covered his face. When he saw Mom he touched the reins and the mule willingly stopped.

"A good morning to you, nice young lady. I have everything you see and more. Sewing needles from England - the best quality, none finer anywhere. I can repair pots and pans and kettles. I sharpen scissors and knives." He looked at the assortment of utensils we were carrying and smiled.

"How much will you charge to fix these?" Mom and I held out our collection.

The Tinker examined each item carefully; setting them down one by one in a neat row on the ledge of his wagon. He frowned thoughtfully, wrinkled his brow and stroked his moustache.

"The kettle I don't fix. To thin, poor quality. If I fix it and soon it leaks you'll say I cheat you and I don't want anyone to say I cheat them. For the rest, fifteen cents each except the loose handle, twenty cents. The scissors? A gift from your Mother?"

"Yes. They need sharpening."

"I can tell scissors. Mothers always give their daughters the best. Twenty cents and they'll cut like new." He held out his hand for the scissors but Mom just stood there with them cradled in her hands.

"That comes to seventy cents. I'm not sure I want to spend that much."

The tinker looked at the row of utensils and then turned back and smiled triumphantly. "Today is slow and I need the work. For you, nice young lady, I'll work extra hard and also fix the kettle for the same price. Then if it ever leaks, such bad luck, you can't say I am no good. What do you say to that? All these fine things fixed up good as new, scissors sharp, all for seventy cents."

The deal was struck. Mom handed over the scissors and the Tinker gathered the items from the ledge and disappeared inside the wagon. Mom went back inside to her housework and I sat on the steps watching and waiting.

At long last the door at the back of the wagon opened and the tinker stepped out. He took off a worn and dirty apron, hung it inside and pulled out our pot, pail, kettle and teakettle. He walked briskly up to the house and I ran inside to tell Mom.

Mom inspected each item and when she was satisfied, counted out the coins into the Tinker's hand.

"It's a warm day; would you like a glass of water?"

"Nice young lady, I would very much like a glass of water."

Mom went back inside and soon returned, carrying a glass of water which she gave to the Tinker. He drank it quickly and handed the glass back to Mom.

"Thank you very much nice young lady. Enjoy your scissors."

We stood and watched as the mule resumed its dulcetory ambulation and the wagon slowly clattered and clinked its way down the street.

After the end of the War I don't think any more tinkers ever appeared. Whenever a pot sprung a leak, Mom would have to buy a repair kit at the dime store but those repairs didn't last very long; with new-found prosperity and aluminum cookware everyone finally resorted to throwing out leaky pots and pans.

Tinkers weren't the only door-to-door businesses in those days. The life insurance salesman came by each month to collect the premiums due. At regular intervals the Jewel Tea man would appear carrying a sample tray full of spices and other household necessities. Then came the Fuller Brush man, followed by the Ice man and the Milk man. During the winter you had groceries and coal or fuel oil delivered. Doctors made house calls. There were gas meter readers and electric meter readers and water meter readers. With that kind of activity there must have someone at the door all the time. It was a way of living that was doomed by the stress it caused to parents of small children.

One warm day our front door was open and I was standing inside the screen door watching all that foot traffic up and down the street when an old woman walked up our sidewalk, smiled and knocked at the door. I turned and hollered as loud as I could, "Mom,

that old biddy that sells magazines is here." I'm sure
Mom lived in terror of knocks at the door for years
afterwards.

Central Elementary School was demolished in 2007 in spite of
a vigorous campaign to save it. There just wasn't any
practical use for the beautiful and solidly built structure.
Photo courtesy Noble County Historical Society.

Fiery Flynn and Others

One of the advantages of growing up in a town like Worthington was the chance to meet and be recognized by so many people. Whenever I walk the streets today I'm reminded again and again of those familiar faces that we saw as youngsters.

Mom and Pop Smith are among the first I remember. Pop ran a barber shop on Tenth Street and Mom - everyone called her Mom so I don't even remember her first name - worked at Cashel's Nursing home. Mom Smith had beautiful silver hair and in the winter wore a light blue coat with a big fluffy fur collar. Once, when their daughters babysat me, I got stung by a bumble bee that had built a nest in an old pump in their backyard. The Smiths were my Godparents.

We lived on Strait Avenue for a while, across the street from Mr. and Mrs. Henry Riss and their large family. They had an old car in the back yard and my brother and I played over there daily. One day Kerry ran home and yelled to Mom that I had "caught the freckles from the Riss's." He must have been right, for to this day I'm still peppered from head to foot.

Mrs. Riss was always an island of calm in a sea of pandemonium. She baked pies for several restaurants - that must have taken special skill with all those kids under foot. Whenever I think of the Riss's or that neighborhood I always hear screen doors banging, dogs barking and kids hollering with delight. With that constant tumult, adults had to remain patient and calm or leave - there was no other choice.

We belonged to St. Mary's Church and Sunday Mass was always full of friendly faces - old men in their shiny, dark wool suits, their names sounding like the Sunday All-saints Litany - Grandpa Flynn, Grandpa O'Brien, Grandpa McCabe, ... When you're little about all you see in a crowd is shiny suits. One Sunday Grandpa Flynn slipped his pipe into his suit coat pocket as he entered church, thinking the pipe was out. He was seated right in front of us so we were able to see the smoke begin to billow out of his pocket just as Father Hale's sermon reached its climax. Someone quickly stripped the smoking coat off a startled Grandpa Flynn, beat out the smudge, and dragged the smoldering remains, like an un-repentant sinner, right down the main aisle and out the front door!

Grandpa O'Brien worked for the Rock Island Railroad and lived right next to the tracks where they crossed West Ninth Avenue. He had one of those little track inspection cars - the kind with the one-lung gas engine that fired with staccato irregularly. When we played by the tracks we would often see him and that car chugging along like a little yellow beetle, popping and puffing merrily. We wondered what he'd do if a train came along. It never occurred to us the he probably knew the schedule - anyway there was only about one train a day.

Chautauqua Park with its lakeshore, band shell, swimming beach, picnic area and large playground kept us busy many summer days. If you spent any time in the city parks then you soon met Hap Ehlers, the Park Superintendent. Hap was a tall man with muscular arms, a slightly rounded stomach, blond hair and face flushed pink by the sun. Hap must have worked hard at keeping those parks looking good, for in fact they were always clean, painted, repaired and loaded with flowers. We always found him clad in a denim shirt and bib overalls with some tool in his hands - raking, pruning, shoveling or sweeping. He was not a jocular man but I think he enjoyed talking to us about his beautiful parks. I'm sure he often instructed us about how to behave in his domain but never with a cross word. His methods must have worked because we took care never to misuse his parks. Hap and Henry Fauskee, the plumber, were the official pancake turners at the Turkey Day Free Pancake Tent.

Mrs. Brown and her son, Reggie, ran a small grocery store at the end of Tenth Street where the new Post Office stands today. My mom would often write up a grocery list and send us off to their store. Everything was behind the counter and they picked out each item for you. If it was too high to reach they had a long pole with a clamp on the end that was used to pluck boxes and cans from the top shelves. When luncheon meat was on the list we were instructed how to order it - "five THIN slices of pimento loaf please." Butcher paper on a large roll and string coming up through a hole in the counter - the paper was pulled and torn with a flourish, deftly folded over the meat, string whipped around twice, tied and snapped. Mrs. Brown always wore a cotton print dress, brown cotton hose and a loose gray sweater - She seemed very old to me and I guess she was - I think by 1950 the store was closed.

After the end of the War, Mr. Barber, who lived down McMillan Street from us, was the most popular man in town - he ran the Studebaker Garage and was the first car dealer to have new cars again. One of his models was the Crosley - a very, very small car that only a few people fit into. We had several of those miniature station wagons buzzing around town for a while. The

Barbers were also the first family in town to get a television set. They installed a tall wooden telephone pole in their back yard and put the antenna on top. For several nights you had to get to their house early to find a spot on the sidewalk where you could see the little round TV screen through their living room window. Since the closest station was in Minneapolis, even a good seat inside would seldom have resulted in a recognizable picture.

Like many kids of that era I had my tonsils out at an early age, I also wore glasses to correct a "lazy eye" - this combination brought me into contact with Dr. Stanley, the eye, ear, nose and throat specialist at the Worthington Clinic. Dr. Stanley's office was always dark - a desk lamp with a green glass shade lit the desktop but left the rest of the office in gloom. The shadowy office, coupled with the collection of eye testing machinery, books, charts, and other paraphernalia, created an atmosphere not unlike that of the movies "mad scientist" laboratory. When left alone in his office I often expected Peter Lorre or Boris Karloff or Bela Lugosi to appear at any moment. Dr. Stanley was a truly gentle doctor but I was always glad to get back into the sunlight.

When Dad needed clothes he always went downtown early in the morning and got to Silverberg's Department Store at opening time. If he was lucky enough to be the first customer in the store that day, Abe Silverberg would personally wait on him. Dad knew that Abe believed making a sale to the first customer in the store was a sign of a good day ahead - this gave Dad tremendous bargaining power and usually resulted in an extra pair of socks or a free tie or belt. When the sale was complete, the money and sales slip where sent whizzing aloft in a small wooden cup suspended on a wire that went from the sales desk up to a cashier's cage on a balcony that overlooked the sales floor. Soon the receipt and change would slide back down the wire. Abe was small and stooped with age. He always patted us on the head and joked with us when we were in the store with Dad. I liked him.

One day in early summer I went with Doug Fiola on a visit to his Grandpa Foss's farm. When we arrived, Grandpa Foss took us to a small fenced-in pasture and presented each of us with a calf. The calves wore halters with a short lead rope attached. Our job, we were told, was to lead those calves around the pasture. As soon as we got a good grip on the rope Grandpa turned the calf loose. We soon found out who was leading - it was not Doug or me. Those calves dragged us all over that pasture as we gamely hung on. I don't know how long we lasted but we were worn out in the end. I guess Grandpa Foss knew how to keep two small boys from getting into mischief on a farm.

Nightingale

Watching trains wasn't my only experience with railroads. We had relatives in Lincoln, Nebraska, and traveled there by train several times. We usually left Worthington in the late afternoon and arrived in Omaha during the night, where we changed from the Chicago & Northwestern to the Burlington Railroad. The trip from Omaha to Lincoln was short but it was still very late at night by the time we got to Aunt Mibs and Uncle Dale's house.

There was a night train that ran between Minneapolis and Omaha called The Nightingale. It arrived in Worthington past midnight and it was early morning when it arrived in Omaha. There were sleeping cars like the ones you see in old movies – double bunks with curtains. Mom tried it once because it was much easier to travel with small, sleeping children. When you're young, time moves very slowly and being cooped up on a train for several hours must have been awful -

I've forgotten that part. What I do remember must give some indication of what it was like to travel by train with little children and why Mom chose the Nightingale! Usually we took the afternoon train which left Worthington around four o'clock and arrived in Omaha at about ten-thirty. Then we'd change trains and arrive in Lincoln at midnight.

The seats where covered with dark green or dark blue mohair and had a foot rest you could pull up. The seat backs had heavy, white cloth covers (antimacassars I think they're called). If you were lucky - or could afford to tip - you could get pillows from the steward. We usually tried to get a pair of seats facing each other, that way my brother and I could both sit by a window. The trains we rode to Omaha started out in St. Paul so getting your choice of seats was doubtful; at every stop people would scramble for more desirable seating arrangements.

Most of my memories revolve around things at the ends of the cars - I suppose that means that I spent most of the trip running back and forth from one end of the car to the other! First was the water cooler with those flimsy pointed paper cups. By the time the train got to Worthington the waste container under the cooler was full and used cups overflowed onto the floor. First we'd drink and then we'd have to go to the toilet.

The toilets were a marvel of simplicity - a bowl with a foot operated trap door that opened directly to the tracks below. You could stand (or sit) right there and watch the ties rush by as you did whatever you had to do. No wonder they locked the toilets before entering a station.

We couldn't afford the dining car but we did get to walk from car to car on the moving train. Whenever someone opened the heavy door at the end of the car the racket would drown out all conversation. The space between two cars was very exciting - the roar of the train, the clatter of steel wheels on steel rails, the creak and groan of the cars against one another, the wind and the smell of coal smoke. Stopping between cars seemed to a very daring thing to do.

After a very long time, we'd be in Lincoln, waiting sleepily for Aunt Mibs to finish making our beds up. I never have figured out how we got from the station to my Aunt and Uncle's house - we must have been sound asleep all the way from Omaha. Those beds weren't too bad either because the next thing you know the smells of breakfast would wake us up.

Days in Lincoln were busy for everyone. Saturday morning we went with my cousin, Suzanne, to her dance class. Suzanne was a good dancer and Aunt Mibs sometimes played the piano at the dance studio where the classes were held. I got a gold star or maybe it was a red dot, anyway I got recognized for something - most likely having come the farthest, certainly not for my dancing prowess. I'm not sure I would have chosen dance lessons as a way to start a visit to Lincoln but we did manage to enjoy ourselves.

In the afternoon, my Uncle Dale would take over and we would have a grand time. I don't know if Uncle Dale enjoyed entertaining us but if he didn't, we never knew it. Those Saturday afternoons were the most exciting adventures a four-year old ever had. First we'd go to the bank where Uncle Dale worked and pick up all the wooden adding machine tape spools that everyone at the bank saved for him. He collected the spools to burn in the stove at his cabin on the Platte River. Next he'd take us to the sunken gardens - these are spectacular flower gardens in a city park that are built in terraces that gradually led down to reflecting pools full of large goldfish. We ran and jumped and enjoyed the sunken gardens.

Then on to the Monkey House. I don't think the Monkey House was big enough to be called a zoo but to us it was like going to Africa or the jungles of Borneo - no animals like this in Worthington! The star was an Orangutan that sat high up in his cage, seeming to ignore everything and everyone around him, until the unwary wandered within range. He could spit with phenomenal range and accuracy. I've heard that they finally had to put glass around his cage to protect the visitors. Birds, snakes, monkeys and other animals all made the visit to the Monkey House exciting.

Back outdoors we'd head for the buffalo park. I've forgotten the official name of the park but remember driving slowly along wooded paths scanning the openings for a glimpse of the shaggy creatures. As soon as we'd spot some, the game was over and we'd head back to civilization - the Museum at the University of Nebraska. There we'd see dinosaur fossils with leg bones bigger than we were. I still have a small bronze triceratops that we bought at the museum.

The last stop was always the State Capitol building with its clean buff limestone and tall graceful tower. There was a small historical museum at the Capitol with Indian artifacts including a skeleton. We'd peer into the glass cases and wonder what it would be like to be an Indian.

I'm sure that by then we were worn down to a manageable state and safe to be taken home. I remember eating supper - they tried to get me to eat peas and fresh tomatoes but I out-waited them. After that it was back to that bed. I don't remember it ever being dark in Lincoln - I was always asleep before dark.

Looking back on those afternoons with Uncle Dale I've come to realize that he was really an artist and taught us much about how to see and appreciate the world around us. We could have been taken to a Saturday afternoon matinee and entertained but learned nothing, instead we got to see and experience natural history, architecture, archeology, zoology and art - and enjoy ourselves more than we ever could at a movie. I do hope he enjoyed those days as much as I did.

Too soon it was time to leave. I remember two incidents connected with going home after visits. The first was being on the platform at the Lincoln depot when the Burlington Zephyr pulled in. The whole train was polished silver - I remember the diesel locomotive as being polished silver too. The engine was bigger and sleeker than anything I'd ever seen - I can still see its big headlight, feel its vibrations, hear its deep rumbling engine. The second incident was being pushed back and forth between trains - we'd get on one and the conductor would tell us it was full, go to the other one. At that train it was the same story. When we finally did get a seat, the train was so late we missed our connection in Omaha. Luckily, Mom heard a ticket clerk tell two WACs that they could catch the train in Council Bluffs if they took a cab across the river - but they'd better hurry. We caught the train - I don't remember the cab ride but Mon always said it was a lulu.

Years later, in August, 1959, I rode one of the last passenger trains through Worthington - two shabby, well-worn passenger cars, a baggage car and several freight cars made up our train. Instead of a dining car, Tex Banister of the Depot Cafe walked up and down the cars selling ham sandwiches and pop. No one bothered to lock the toilets when we pulled into a station. We didn't even go to the Union Depot in Omaha - the train stopped in the middle of the freight yard in Council Bluffs, Iowa, and we walked across several sets of tracks to a waiting city bus and rode it to the Union Deport in Omaha. It seemed like the sorry little train was too embarrassed to be seen in a place as grand as the Omaha Union Depot.

Going back to revisit the Sunken Gardens in Lincoln has long been on my Bucket List! Luckily, I recently had an opportunity to visit Lincoln, made a special effort go find the park containing those gardens and discovered them to be even lovelier that I remembered.

How to Hypnotize a Chicken

When we moved there, McMillan Street was paved as far as Clary and was cinders from there on north. All of the major highways ran through downtown, so the only traffic past our house was either headed out into the country or down Clary Street - there wasn't much traffic by our house. At the other end of McMillan, where it joins Tenth Street and Tenth Avenue, Albinson's Lumber Yard, St. John's elevator, the Rock Island freight depot, Bass grocery, Brown's store and a turkey hatchery were the hub of our urban world.

Living at the edge of town with a railroad, grain elevator and turkey hatchery meant that animals, both domestic and wild, were all around us. We'd catch chickens that escaped from the trucks stopped at the grain elevator - Mom made a very tasty stewed chicken. We learned how to hypnotize a chicken by holding its head to the ground and drawing a line from its eye with our finger. When you'd let go it couldn't move!

When turkeys were hatching the weak ones were thrown outside the hatchery into a large wagon. We rescued several and tried to revive them but I don't remember having home-grown turkey for thanksgiving, so I don't think we ever succeeded. We raised a baby robin though, thanks to Mom's skill as a nurse and her use of buttermilk.

One day I found a nest of baby garter snakes, put them in a coffee can and brought them home. I put the can on top of our ice box and forgot about it. In those days one pound coffee cans were shorter and wider than today - no problem at all for a dozen small snakes. Our telephone hung on the wall above the ice box.

The telephone rang.

Mom answered and, as she did, looked down at the top of the icebox finding herself gazing at a tangle of slithering and writhing snakes.

I guess Mom had nightmares about snakes for quite a while after that - the sight of all those wiggling snakes on top of the ice box must have made quite an impression on her. She made an impression on me too - I never brought more than one snake at a time home after that.

I tried another tack and brought home a family of field mice complete with nest. No luck - as soon as Mom found them I had to throw them out too. My brother, Kerry, brought home a sick red tailed hawk. He fed it for a few days until it got better and flew away - at least he had some success with wild animals.

On the West side of our street was a farm run by a man named Bristol, whose fields extended all the way to the Diagonal Road. Mr. Bristol was a taciturn and business-like man and we never saw much of him except at work in his fields. He had horses and we often watched him working with them - mowing, raking and cultivating. North of his farm, where Whiskey Ditch runs under McMillan, there was a small shed where another farmer kept a pair of mules. In the spring we had our garden plowed by those mules. They were used regularly to perform other tasks in the neighborhood - digging basements, hauling trees, pulling down old sheds. Whenever we heard jangling harness and rhythmic hoof beats, we'd troop along like Hamelin's children after the piper, to see what new project was in store for those mules.

The Ice Man also had a horse to pull his wagon. As he went from house to house we'd follow him and marvel at how deftly he could split a large block of ice with just a few well-placed stabs from his pick. Sometimes we'd pick up chips of ice and he'd rinse them off for us with water he carried in a large drum on the back of the wagon. Our mothers warned us not to eat that ice - "it's just frozen lake water - who knows what's in it - you'll get sick for sure." Of course by then the ice plant by Lake Okabena used refrigeration machinery to make those blocks of ice so no lake water. When we did get sick it wasn't from eating lake ice - more likely from eating too many green apples. The garbage man also used a horse drawn wagon - we never followed the garbage wagon.

When animal entertainment was scarce we'd head for the old fairgrounds - along Clary Street where the high school is now. There was a large barn there where horses were kept. The doors were always open and we could wander in and out as we pleased. Sometimes a friendly soul would let us help feed, water, hold reins and such. When we got tired of that we'd sneak under the old grandstand and climb into the scaffolding that supported the seats. Playing in the dim shadows amid the beams and poles worked small boy's imaginations overtime. We'd dream of finding fat billfolds or bulging purses dropped during the fair. The sound of other voices in the gloom would send us scrambling wildly outside - barely escaping a terrible fate at the hands of a band of fierce bullies - who were probably running in the other direction for the same reason. The local baseball team played their games in the infield at the grandstand. We'd play in the seats during their practice sessions but spent the games under the grandstand - still hoping for that falling billfold. I seem to remember that Satchel Page pitched there in an exhibition game.

During our first summer on McMillan, my friend, David Ulrich, and I learned to ride bicycles, or rather learned to ride his older brother's bike. Both of us were too small to get on or off so we'd push the bike to a handy porch, climb aboard and start off - at least our first falls were on grass. After a while we could make it all the way to the street. Now getting off became a real problem. Our only choice was to pick a soft spot and crash land. The only injury I got was when my brother Kerry found out that I'd ripped the seat out of his favorite blue-jeans sliding off the seat of that bicycle - I was wearing his because I'd already ripped the seat out of mine. By the time Aunts Marge and Kay sent my brother and me their old bikes I could ride pretty well.

St. John's elevator caught fire on a bitterly cold night, December 30, 1946. I guess they were drying corn and something got too hot. The elevator burned through and all the corn and beans spilled out into a gigantic flaming mountain - the smoke was so thick you couldn't see. Kerry and I had war surplus gas masks that we used to play "army" with, so in the morning we put them on and headed for the fire. Everything was soot-gray and covered with ice. Steam, smoke and flames rose from the wrecked elevator and the grain pile. Firemen played streams of water aimlessly over the blasted ruins - without much effect. At Brown's store we saw several firemen, coated head to foot with ice, each sitting on a chair in wash tub with their feet in another tub. The firemen sat and drank hot coffee as their ice coating melted into the tubs. The grain pile smoldered for several days so we gave those gas masks a pretty good work out.

As with us, there were many families moving in and out on McMillan. When a family down the street headed for California they announced that everything would be sold at auction, including a beautiful red two-wheeled scooter in perfect condition. I really wanted that scooter. When the auction day came, I headed down the street with all my life savings in my pants pocket, my jaw set and a positive attitude. I stood right in front of the hay wagon used as platform by the auctioneer and his helpers. I held my fire and clutched my money as croquet sets, steel lawn chairs, a baby buggy, garden tools, dishes, laundry tubs came and went.

At last they brought the scooter up onto the wagon. I must have tipped my hand because the auctioneer leaned down and asked me if I was going to bid on the scooter.

I nodded and said I was.

He asked how much money I had.

I told him three dollars.

The auctioneer then stood up, said they had a three dollar bid on the scooter and, before anyone could raise the bid, pronounced it "sold to the little boy in the front."

I've had a fondness for auctions ever since.

A Fair in Time

I remember Augusts in Worthington as quiet and dry. The bright green of June and July becomes deep forest green and the shadows are black under the trees. Everything slows down - you could walk down town during the middle of the day and not see a soul. Sounds faded away except for the chirping of the sparrows fluttering in the dust and flying in and out of the open doors at the grain elevators and lumber yards. I remember when another kid and I rode our bikes to Reading - we must have been so bored that riding 12 miles on a hot summer day was the most exciting thing we could think of.

Whisky ditch would be just a few shallow pools late in the summer and the crayfish have built little mounds of mud around their indoor pools. If there are any carp left, they are easy to catch in the puddles. The thistles are sharp and tall, most of their flowers are seed pods and the goldfinches are having a feast. We could follow the path along the ditch, hidden by those tall thistles, until we would get to the little Rock Island Railroad culvert over the ditch. If our timing was right the afternoon freight train would be heading north to Reading, Wilmont and Lismore and we would duck into the culvert and shout at each other as it clattered overhead. I still miss the sound of a steam train whistle on hot summer night.

After watching the train waddle away we could either follow the ditch trail out of town toward the Febus Dairy dump or take the railroad tracks toward the lake. By August the lake is pea green and smells pretty rotten, besides there's nothing going on at the turkey hatchery, lumber yard or grain elevator so the walk to the lake would be pretty dull.

We'd usually follow the ditch all the way to the place where it goes under the highway. This was a big concrete box culvert with mud a foot deep and very soft - you take your shoes off and slide your toes into the cool pudding like muck, expecting broken glass or an angry crayfish or a hungry snapping turtle. Now that was excitement! The barn swallow nests on the concrete walls were empty and the culvert made a nice echo as you splashed and squished your way through.

The banks are wider on the other side of the culvert and Okabena Creek north of Whisky Ditch is dry. Tall grass and nettles replace the thistles - farmers spray thistles and we are in farm fields now. The corn is way over our head, sharp, stiff and dusty. The weeds along the fences are dry and full of sticky seeds. Milkweed pods are big but not ripe yet - the plants are stiff but still ooze white sap when you break a leaf. Maybe you can spot a jade green, jeweled monarch butterfly chrysalis (I've seen very few monarchs again this year, we need more butterfly gardens). The open country is quiet and the farm yards empty. The summer work is done - no more hay, the oats and barley are long into bins, the last cultivating was weeks ago, only the ubiquitous sparrows inhabit the barns and sheds.

Silent machines sit in the shade, old binders and thrashing machines, horse drawn dump rakes and cultivators, wooden wheeled wagons, planters, drags, plows. Some are in neat rows, some strewn randomly in the shady grove - many never to move again except to Shapiro's scrap yard - a lucky few may end up on display to remind us of our fading rural past. Where had their masters gone? It's too late in the summer to fish, ball games are done, no one ever traveled very far then - maybe they, too, were sitting in the shade waiting for fall, like waiting for school to start just so there'd be some action.

Up the ditch, off to the northwest was the Febus Dairy dump. Milk bottles that failed to pass muster were heaped in piles there. If you looked carefully you could find some that still looked useable, or at least looked useable enough to get you a nickel at Bass's Market after they'd been washed. I don't remember how we got the bottles home; we must have taken our shirts off and used them as sacks. We probably blew the money on candy. Maybe we saved it for the County Fair but I doubt it.

The Nobles County Fair - noise, crowds, lights, motion, what a relief from the silence - where did those crowds of people come from? Had they spent weeks in their basements building up their strength and courage to face the tilt-a whirl? The Grandstand Show was "Joie Chitwood and his Auto Dare-devils" with Percy the Clown - I guess we all got our money's worth on that one.

Mom says I once laughed so hard at Percy's antics that people were laughing at me as much as at the clown! I can still see Percy's bib overalls fall down as an old Chevrolet teetering on two wheels came roaring past, just missing everything but Percy's overalls. I still laugh at that memory.

To us youngsters, the most fascinating attraction at the fairgrounds was the self-flushing toilets! You didn't have to pay but you did have to have patience. A small pipe fed a steady stream of water into a large barrel which had a pivot toward its bottom. When the barrel filled with water it finally became top heavy and emptied with a roar, sending a wall of water rushing down a sluice trough that ran under the stalls - what a sight! Not exactly the Glockenspiel on the City Hall in Munich but pretty high tech for a small prairie town.

Maybe that's why August is quiet - we all seek the shade and fade into past Augusts, remembering those long shadows in the morning, clear dry days, green apples suddenly sweet, a time when everyone was waiting for the fair.

Joie Chitwood and his Auto Daredevils were frequent performers at the old Nobles County Fairgrounds located on Clary Street where the high school now stands.

Moon Dream

Dark. Velvet black void dark. Nothing visible inside the barn, not the dirt floor, not the wooden walls, not the stalls, not your hands; nothing but darkness. Thin needles of silver moonlight pierce through gaps in the walls making silver daggers in the dirt. Slender silver daggers lying dimly on the dirt, like animal eyes that watch coldly in the darkness.

You crouch, silent, listening, waiting, unseen and unseeing. Try to move to the light, to the silver daggers' beckoning glimmer. It's so hard to move, you reach out for the light but get no closer; you crawl silently in the gloomy cavern of the barn, crawl to the light but cannot reach it. Why is it so hard to crawl? You need to go to the light. Yes, go to the light. It's safe, safe in the light.

Is It in the far recesses of the night filled barn? Can you feeling It lingering in the shadows? What is It that waits for you in the black void? What terrible want does

It have for you? How do you know It's there? What is It that terrifies you so? Be quiet and It may not notice you. Don't move and It may not hear you.

Smell the dust and the straw and the animal smell. The air in the barn is heavy and still. Breathe slowly. It's hard to breathe; the heavy air is hard to breathe. You gag on each breath, hardly able to inhale in your growing terror. You've become so stiff with fright you cannot move; but you must move, you must flee, you must reach the light. It comes closer, you know It comes closer, comes for you in the dark. Your hands are in the soft dry powder dirt of the barn floor but you feel nothing. The dirt is soft as air. Why can't you feel the dirt? You touch the walls, the rough board walls. They are there but your fingers must be too numb to feel them. Maybe there is a door in the wall; maybe you can find a doorway to the light. Feel the walls, feel for a doorway. Faster, move faster, It comes closer, you know It comes closer in the soft darkness. The barn is so large, the walls go on and on without doors or corners, on and on into the black with only the moonlight daggers on the floor. Your heart pounds faster and faster. If only you could get up and run, run to the light, run away from the clinging night. Get up and run away from It! You can't get up. You crawl slowly, pressing your hands down onto the dirt. Why can't you feel the dirt? It's so close now! It surrounds you, envelops you! Flee! You must flee! You must escape to the light.

Feel; feel the smooth cloth, slowly slide your hand across the smooth cloth. Are you asleep? Do you feel the sheet? Does your head press against a pillow? Yes, you're asleep. No! Now you're awake and in bed. Yes, awake.

Awake! A dream! Are you awake? Was it a dream? You're drenched with sweat, the sheet clings like a shroud, your heart hammers in your ears and you're gasping for air. You must be awake.

Raise your head and open your eyes. Nothing visible, nothing but darkness. Thin needles of silver moonlight pierce through gaps in the curtains making silver daggers on the floor. Slender silver daggers lying dimly on the floor, like animal eyes that watch coldly in the darkness.

#

How does an eight year old boy dream such dreams and then wake up to such a frightening reality? Even today I can relive every sensation of that terrible nightmare and the terror I felt after waking up to find myself in the dark moonlight alone in the bedroom. I slid down under the covers in panic and finally returned to a dreamless sleep that lasted until morning.

Three Fish Tales

I was so bored by winters on Twelfth Street that I remember little about them, except melting color crayons in the living room stove and my glasses steaming over when I got home from school. Spring is a different story though; all my pent up energy of winter must have exploded in the spring for, like dandelions, my spring memories pop up everywhere.

In the spring of 1945 the level of Lake Okabena was unusually high. Water ran several inches deep over the outlet spillway, turning it into a miniature Niagara Falls. On the other side of the Chicago and Northwestern railroad tracks the rushing torrent emerged from two large tunnels and emptied into a drainage ditch that eventually ends up in Lake Ocheda. Word of this rare watery phenomena spread quickly and both places were soon crowded with sightseers enjoying the unfamiliar sight and sound of the cataracts. No doubt the crowd included sharp-eyed sportsmen who quickly discovered schools of bullheads massed just below the outlet pipes in the ditch. The current in the ditch must have attracted the fish from Lake Ocheda and their wanderlust drew them to the barrier they now confronted. Unable or unwilling to turn back, a giant tangle of bullheads wiggled and splashed on both sides of the ditch.

We followed some older boys - the Basche brothers I think - to the banks of the ditch below the outlet. Now I must confess that normally we were not permitted anywhere near older boys. After all, how can teenagers impress whoever needs impressing if they are being followed around by grade schoolers generally acting like a bunch of little puppy dogs. At rare moments our idols let down their guard and we basked in the glow of their attention. The Basches' had a pigeon loft in the old barn behind their house. Once in a while we were allowed to help with feeding the pigeons and were even allowed to hold a bird - what joy. I don't know why we were allowed along on the trip to see the bullheads in the ditch; at moments like that we didn't ask too many questions.

When the hardy band arrived at the ditch bank our fearless leaders took of their shirts, shoes and socks and waded into the bullhead swarm. Putting their hands together they began to scoop bullheads up onto the bank. The water was so thick with fish that several ended up flapping on the grass with each scoop. Our job was to grab the prey before they could flop their way back into the water. We pounced, being careful to avoid those sharp spines, and slid the unfortunate quarry onto stringers that had been brought along by the older boys for just that purpose.

When the stringers were full, a procession headed triumphantly homeward with the older boys marching proudly at the head and us younger ones struggling along behind dragging the heavy stringers. We didn't complain - in fact we were delighted to carry the fish - it made us feel big too.

Once home the big boys - and their mother too I'll bet - set about cleaning the fish and collecting the meat in a large galvanized washtub. After the cleaning was done the whole troop reassembled and went door-to-door around the neighborhood selling fresh bullheads for a penny each. I seem to remember that the young assistants each received a dime for their efforts. The satisfaction of being allowed to help our idols was worth far more than a dime.

* * *

A few springs later, Ronnie White and I are lying atop the White's chicken coop, on the warm shingles, protected from the cool spring breeze behind the peak of the roof, armed to the teeth with Ronnie's BB gun; waiting like big game hunters for any sparrow the might fly into the box elder tree next to the chicken coop and land within range of the BB gun. A shout from the back porch and we are scrambling down from the roof and running to the house - all thoughts of sparrow hunting have quickly disappeared. We have been invited on a big game safari of sorts.

Ronnie's long, lean older brothers lead the way. We walk fast to keep up with those long-legged strides, giving us little time to imitate the easy saunter that teenage boys have. The procession heads north along the Rock Island Railroad tracks, Ronnie and I balancing on the rails and skipping from tie to tie. The brothers each carry a .22 caliber rifle, Ronnie and I a gunny sack.

At the place where Whiskey Ditch goes under the railroad tracks we leave civilization behind and plunge into the wilderness, following the trail that leads along the bank towards the Diagonal Road. Just short of Highway 16 we stop and set up camp at a spot where the water in the ditch is shallow enough to see the bottom.

Our prey is the large black suckers that foolishly swim over those shallows. The sharp-eyed brothers stand on the bank and wait with deadly stealth, taking care not to move lest they reveal their sinister intent to the fish. We also stand statue still, barefoot and ready for action. When a fish appears there is a quick shot and then a mad scramble as Ronnie and I jump into the water to grab the mortally wounded fish and throw it up on the bank before it slides back into deeper water. The marksman retrieves his prey and drops it into his sack. I don't know if the fish wised up to what was happening or if the brothers had simply shot all that were there; but at last the action dies down and the shooting is over. We break camp and head back to town with Ronnie and me each carrying a gunny sack of dead fish. I don't remember how they cooked those suckers - maybe that's just as well.

Ronnie and I climb back atop the chicken coop and resume our patient and deadly wait; now pretending to be older brothers and imagining the sparrows to be fish.

Bullheads never again were an important factor in my early years but I did have another encounter with a black sucker and sort of came out a loser.

* * *

We left Worthington in 1948, moved to Mason City, Iowa, and our new home there was only a few blocks from Willow Creek which runs right through downtown

Mason City. I spent a lot of time playing down at the creek and fishing along its banks.

A small neighborhood grocery stood right next to the creek and we'd often beg scraps from the grocer to use as bait. First we'd tie on a piece of pimento loaf and catch several crawfish. Then we'd put a hook on the line, bait it with fresh crawfish tail and go after bigger game. Mostly we just caught more crawfish and once in a while a small turtle; only rarely would we get any fish.

One morning I headed down to the creek by myself and started fishing from a small bridge next to the grocery store. I don't know how long I waited but it couldn't have been long because I don't think I could stay put in one spot for very long at that age. I felt a mighty tug on my line, set the hook and battled a large black sucker into submission - reeling the fish straight up out of the water and onto the bridge.

Eager to share my excitement and to brag about my fishing prowess, I marched into the grocery store proudly holding up the fish for all to see.

A lady stood waiting at the counter as the grocer totaled up her purchases. "What a nice fish," she said to me. "What are you going to do with it?"

"I don't know," I replied.

In fact I did know - Mom made us bury all the fish we caught in the garden after my brother and his friends brought home a pail full of crawfish that they planned to sell, put them in the garage and forgot all about them until the neighborhood began to take on the odor of dead fish.

"I'll give you a dime for it."

I handed her the fish and took the dime.

"I won't be needing this," she said to the grocer and reached over to the counter, picked up a package of frozen Ocean Perch from among her purchases and put it back in the freezer case.

After the lady left the store I learned a valuable lesson about biting the hand that feeds you. The grocer ordered me off the premises and vowed to never give any of us kids any scraps for bait ever again if all we were going to do was come in his store and take away his business by selling fish that he helped us catch at such ridiculously low prices how was he supposed to make a living anyway.

I don't think we ever had a chance to sell any other fish after that but I never took another fish into the grocery store again either.

The Best Christmas Ever

"Be sure and bring a glass jar to school Monday," said Miss Seibring, my third grade teacher. "We're going to make pencil holders for Christmas presents."

With that announcement, Thanksgiving, 1946, at Worthington Central Elementary School was over, the drawings of pilgrims and Indians and turkeys and pumpkins were taken down from above the blackboard and we went to work creating new decorations - snowmen and sleighs and Christmas trees and red Santa's and snowflakes.

"We're making pencil holders," I told my older brother, Kerry, as we walked home from school. "I have to bring a jar to school."

"I'm making an ashtray out of clay with marbles in it."

Our overshoes ground noisily through the snow in the alley. We always took the alleys home from school, journeys that provided us with an ever changing display, artifacts arrayed in trash cans or leaning forlornly against some shed - broken radios, bicycles without wheels, three legged chairs, rusty bed springs. In our bulky brown coats, stocking caps, overshoes and mittens we must have looked like a pair of bear cubs as we wandered along peering into burning barrels, turning over boards or tugging at objects frozen into the snow.

As we started up the last alley, Spot came running around the bushes behind our house, snow flying, ears flapping and tail wagging.

"Hey! Spot!" Kerry yelled. Spot barked in reply.

Spot was Kerry's dog. Kerry found him early that spring, sick and starving and brought him home. Mom didn't want to let Spot stay but he stayed anyway. Now he was our best friend. Every morning he'd follow us to that same place, watch till we disappeared and then walk slowly homeward, head down, tail dragging. He was glad to see that we'd come back safely from another day a school.

Kerry pulled a stick out of a fence and threw it up the alley. "Fetch," he shouted.

Spot ran up the alley, almost catching the stick before it hit the ground. He stopped and waited for us to catch up to him. We walked a little faster with Spot along; like us, his work was done and he was eager to get home and play.

It was already getting dark by the time we reached our house. The fading light made the snow blue and turned the shadows black. We pushed open the back door and stepped into the warm, moist, golden light of the kitchen. My glasses steamed up as always. Spot shook himself.

"Where have you two been?" Mom asked without turning away from the sink. She was peeling potatoes. "Dad has to leave at five so we're going to eat right away."

Dad played the trumpet in an orchestra. During the holidays, the orchestra played almost every night. That meant Dad was usually gone by the time we got home from school.

We pulled off our mittens and coats as quickly as we could and then kicked off our overshoes - leaving our school shoes inside. We ran and slid across the linoleum in our stockings. Dad was in the bedroom getting dressed.

"Gotcha." Dad picked us up, one in each arm, as we ran into the bedroom. "How's School?"
"I need a jar," I said without thinking about the secrecy of the present.

"When can we come along again?" Kerry asked. The previous summer Dad had taken us along with the orchestra to a dance, we wanted to go again.

"Boys! Come and help set the table."

Dad set us down and we ran to the kitchen. Mom handed Kerry the plates and told me to get the silverware. I liked to put silverware on the table - fork on the left, knife and spoon on the right; neat, balanced and orderly, and a baby spoon on Tim's high chair. Tim is my little brother.

"We'll get a tree tomorrow morning. The band is playing at Valhalla so I don't have to leave until seven-thirty. There's a tree lot across from the Post Office and it looks like they have nice ones."

I looked at Kerry and he grinned, Tim banged his spoon on his plate. We were going downtown tomorrow! What fun! I don't think Mom and Dad shared our enthusiasm, it would be crowded and slushy and they'd be herding two and carrying one and we had to walk both ways.

"I'm taking the baby buggy. If we're going shopping I'm not carrying Tim and groceries too." Mom put a bowl of mashed potatoes on the table and went back to the stove for the codfish gravy.

We hated codfish gravy but the salted codfish came in a little wooden box with a sliding lid, a perfect box for keeping treasures in. I wondered whose turn it was to get the box. Maybe it was my turn to get the box. "I get the box."

"You got it last time," Kerry said.

"I get it this time." Dad held up the box.

Kerry looked at me and I looked at him. I think both of us felt we'd won - if one didn't get the box the other didn't either! At least the codfish gravy didn't have peas in it.

"You don't have to take the buggy, we're not walking home. Franky Anderson is going to meet us at the Adams Hotel. We can leave everything we buy there till we're done."

Franky Anderson drove the cab. We were going to take the cab home! Now that was going to be a trip, downtown shopping and then a cab ride home - we still had to walk downtown though.

* * *

Evergreen rope snaked up around every light post and telephone pole, red stars surrounded by large wreaths swung gaily, held up by ropes festooned with colored lights. Through steamy storefront windows we could see all the Christmas delights; at Johnson's Bakery, shiny coffee cakes studded with cherries and pecans lounged seductively, chocolate samplers of all sizes waited lovingly at Ahlf's Drug Store, plaster boys with wool sweaters and corduroy pants looked warm and happy in Habicht's, a pioneer village of Lincoln Logs stood next to an Erector Set amusement park at the Ben Franklin Store.

Kerry and I looked carefully at the Lincoln Logs. We hoped Mom and Dad were watching.

What should we get Grandma Dewey? Mom suggested bath powder. And Grandma McCauley? Dad thought a box of chocolates would be just right. Shopping was easy when your mom and dad had all the answers - and the money.

Kerry went with Dad so Mom and Tim and I went down to Dingler's Sporting Goods. Kerry was in fourth grade and liked to build model airplanes out of balsawood and tissue paper. At Dingler's I bought him a model airplane kit, it had a rubber band engine and cost forty-nine cents.

At last the shopping was done and we headed for the Post Office. The Kiwanis had a tree lot across the street at the John Deere Implement lot. Tractors and manure spreaders and pig feeders and Christmas trees all in one spot. There were huge piles of trees, tied in tight bundles. A few trees were untied and leaning against the tractors. They were all balsams, tall, straight, slender and light green, with flat needles. The untied ones were for show so Mom and Dad had to choose one off the pile. We'd have to wait till we got home before we could untie it and see what it looked like. If they'd made a good choice it would be straight and not have any missing branches.

After buying the tree we walked through the alley past Montgomery Wards and Meier's Pool Hall to the Adams Hotel. Kerry and I proudly carried the tree, pretending we cut it ourselves. When we got to the hotel we stayed outside to guard the tree.

"Hi Steve," said the desk clerk as Dad disappeared inside followed by Mom and Tim. Soon Franky came out and opened the trunk of the taxi which was parked right in front of the hotel. Mom and Dad, laden with boxes and bags, followed Franky to the trunk. Almost everything fit, what didn't went into the back seat. The tree was tied on top with twine, running over the roof and right through the open doors. Kerry and Dad and I all rode in the front, there was barely room for Mom and Tim in the back among the packages.

* * *

Dad untied the tree and put it in a pail of warm water - helps the branches come out he says. My Dad knows just about everything I guess.

Mom came up from the basement carrying an old suitcase. She had to carry it with both hands because the handle's broken and the latches won't stay shut. In the living room she opened the case, tissue wrapped ornaments bulged upward and strings of lights uncoiled as if waking up from a long, long sleep.

"One's broken." Mom carefully lifted a crumpled tissue full of broken ornament. "Happens every year no matter how I pack them. Seems like it's always a nice one too."

Everyone started pulling ornaments and lights out of the case. We stopped when we reached the packets of foil icicles.

Dad went into the bedroom and shut the door. He's going to practice his trumpet. He practiced every day. I think he knows just when he has to do it. Seeing those icicles must have made him realize how much he needed that practice.

Mom gave Kerry and I each a pack of icicles.

"When I was a little girl in Primrose, we had the most beautiful tree you ever saw. We spent six days just putting icicles on it. The whole tree was silver, it was lovely."

"Now you have to be very careful. Hang them evenly on the branches. Just like this." Mom slowly pulled a long silver foil icicle from off the top of the pack and hung it over a branch.

Dad puts a mute in the trumpet when he practices. We could hear him playing scales and triple-tonguing exercises. We hung icicles - millions of icicles. Why did I always break mine when I lifted them off the pack? Mom just said to be more careful.

When we started working on the tree the living room was bright and sunny. In our concentration, the slowly fading light went unnoticed until the last icicle was hung and we stepped back to admire our creation. The afternoon sunlight had deepened into a rosy glow and the tree glittered like it was burning fiery red.

Mom plugged in the first string of lights; nothing, not a flicker, not a wink, not a blink.

"If it wasn't so dangerous I'd go back to candles. When I was a little girl in Primrose we had candles on our tree. On Christmas morning my dad would fill every pail we had with water and then light the candles. He would only let them burn for a few minutes. My dad was very, very careful. The whole tree glittered with those candles. It was lovely."

Mom slowly worked her way along the string of lights, snapping each bulb with the tip of her finger. Whenever there would be a brief flicker of life from the string, out would come the bad bulb and in would go a new one. She kept snapping until at last the room was alive with colored light. We helped Mom wind the strings around the tree. Dad stopped practicing and came out to help hang the ornaments.

By the time it was dark the tree was done, a wonderful vision that made Christmas came alive again.

* * *

I remembered to take a jar to school; I had to ask Mom for one. She didn't ask what it was for. I was glad she didn't, it would have been hard to think of a reason I had to take a jar to school. Kerry didn't have to ask for marbles, he already had those.

We took colored crepe paper, tore it into little pieces and soaked in warm salt water. Then we used a fork to press the wet paper around the jar. When the paper dried it was rock-hard and made the jar look like it was covered with colored candy. Miss Seibring helped us paint the rim red for added color. We wrapped our jars in Christmas paper and made tags out of red paper. We wrote "TO MOM AND DAD" in green crayon on the tags and tied them to the package with red yarn.

On the last day of school before Christmas vacation we all brought treats. I talked Mom into popcorn balls - red and green ones. I know she'll never let me do that to her again. I didn't know what a big mess making twenty popcorn balls would be; I guess Mom didn't know either. We popped popcorn, boiled corn syrup, greased our hands with butter and waded in. We stuck to everything, the popcorn stuck to everything, the syrup hardened in the kettle and we had to fight to avoid making only one great big popcorn ball! Only Spot enjoyed the project - he got to lick up the warm, sweet, sticky treats that we dropped to the floor.

On Sunday night we walked to Church for the Christmas program. Dad's orchestra went on a three day trip to South Dakota so Mom took us. Dad wouldn't be home until Christmas Eve.

* * *

Christmas Eve! Our favorite day; Dad was always home that night and we'd all be together. We don't open presents until Christmas Morning, after Santa Claus comes; so Christmas Eve was a time of candy and sweet wine and stories and listening to the radio.

Kerry and I woke up early to the ominous sound of the wind moaning through the bushes and rattling the storm windows. We pulled the curtains aside and peered through the frosted window. Snow! Great heaps of snow! Clouds of snow, billowing and blowing; blotting everything out.

"Mom! It's snowing," we both yelled and ran for the kitchen. "Is Dad home? What will we do?" Before she could answer we ran into the living room and jumped up on the couch so we could see the outside. The street was invisible, hidden by the white maelstrom. This couldn't be! Where's Dad! How will he get home!

"Come to breakfast. Dad will get home. Don't worry."

We trudged disbelievingly to the kitchen where large bowls of hot oatmeal waited to cheer us up. Mom always put a small pat of butter in the oatmeal so it melts and floats around in the milk in little yellow islands. We had toast with orange marmalade. I don't like marmalade; it tastes like orange peeling and makes my tongue wrinkle.

"What if Dad can't come home? What then?" I wanted to know what's going to happen. If Dad can't get here then maybe no one, not even Saint Nick, could get here! "What then?"

"He hasn't called so everything must be alright. It's early. They won't be here for a long time yet. Get dressed and go play."

We weren't convinced. We did get dressed and go down the basement. A few weeks before, Kerry found a coil of strange looking cord stuck between the floor joists in the basement and we'd been experimenting with it. Somehow we discovered that it burned quite nicely. To take our minds off the blizzard we took small pieces of this rope, lit them and dropped them in the basement toilet bowl. To our delight and amazement it kept burning, even under water. At our tender age we didn't know dynamite fuse when we saw it. Mom and

Dad were lucky the previous home owner didn't leave anything but the fuse for us to experiment with.

The storm continued unabated. We could see our lovely Christmas slowly drifting over, sinking into a white ocean to be forever lost. We were overcome with the lethargy of despair.

"Who wants to help make fudge?" Mom called down the basement stairs.

Fudge? I'd forgotten about making candy! Dad would have to struggle along without me for a while. "ME! Can I test to see when it's ready?" The lucky tester got to eat the soft blobs left over from the testing.

"Yes. You can test but only if you help beat it. Kerry, you can help me mix it up."

Soon we stood like Macbeth's witches on the blasted heath, cackling over a boiling cauldron. We'd forgotten the blizzard, forgotten Dad's peril. Mom handed me a large spoon and held out a cup full of cold water. I dipped out a spoonful and poured it into the cup. The water turned chocolate.

"Oh my, that has a long way to go. Keep watching and don't let it boil over."

Finally, a soft fudge ball appeared at the bottom of the cup. Mom turned off the fire and put some butter in the kettle. We now settled down to wait for it to cool.

Mom didn't say anything but we saw her go into the living room and pull the curtains away from the window. She stood quietly for a moment and then let the curtain slide back. Our hearts sank. There hadn't been a phone call all morning, no cars had been down the street, and the snow was blowing harder than ever. Not even beating fudge could take our minds off the storm now.

Morning ticked away and afternoon dragged in. Mom tried her best. The house smelled of cranberries and pumpkin and cinnamon. At last she said, "I guess I'll make divinity." Kerry and I looked at each other, nodded in unison and headed back to the basement to continue our experiments with the dynamite fuse. We'd seen Mom make divinity before and wanted no part of it, blizzard or no blizzard.

Make no mistake, my mother was a very good cook, her Grandmother Russell was a famous cook in Manhattan (actually Manhattan, Kansas), my grandmother and Mom's namesake, Lillian Dewey, was also a cook of fine reputation. I'm sure both of these women could create cloud-like mounds of delicious divinity candy, divinity that melted in your mouth like warm ice cream. Someplace in my mother's past, someone had placed a divinity curse on the family and it stuck on my mother.

Huddled in the protection of the basement toilet bunker we could only imagine the torture that Mom was enduring upstairs. Using all her culinary skills she would carefully cook the candy until just the exact moment and then religiously follow the instructions to beat the cooked confection into airy white perfection.

When we heard the crash of kettle and spoon in the sink we knew the ordeal had reached its climax. Mom had gently ladled dollops of divinity onto sheets of waxed paper, convinced that this time, at last, it had turned out just right. At that point the evil curse slowly dissolved those wonderful, light confections into flat, shiny pools of sticky gook. It looked like someone had poured little puddles of milk of magnesia all over the counter.

"I must be crazy. I don't even like divinity. What makes me do it every year?" Turning around Mom saw Spot standing patiently in front of the ice box.

Spot was no fool. He knew disaster for Mom often meant triumph for Spot. His faith was borne out.

"Here! Merry Christmas!" Mom threw a sheet of white spotted waxed paper on the floor.

Spot managed to eat every piece of candy and the waxed paper too. He did have a little trouble with the paper sticking to the roof of his mouth but he just kept working at it.

Afternoon too was sliding by; still no word from Dad. Drifts piled up in front of the living room window, we had to climb onto the couch to see over them. The street was empty, only the winter wind moved outside the window. As we watched, a sort of melancholy gradually robbed us of all our energy. Even Spot lay quietly by the door and listened to the wind. Mom started to darn socks. Tim slept in his crib. Someone turned on the Christmas tree lights. Bing Crosby sang "White Christmas" over and over on the radio. We watched and waited.

No watcher caught sight of the hunched-over shape plowing step by step up the deserted street. Thump! Spot's ears twitched and he stood up. The front door burst open with a blast of cold air and snow. Dad jumped inside, slamming the door behind him.

We whooped for joy at the sight of Dad standing there covered with snow like Santa Claus. Christmas was here after all!

"I knew it as soon as I left." Dad pulled off his cap and slapped it against his leg, knocking the snow off. "Every time we go on the road and I leave my overshoes home it snows."

"How did you get Home? Why didn't you call? We'd given up."

"We were stuck in Adrian until a snow plow came along. We followed him all the way to Worthington. He came right down Diagonal Road. I jumped off the bus at Bass's Market. They were already closed so I couldn't call. Boy are my feet cold."

We had oyster stew for supper. Dad says they always had it after Midnight Mass when he was a boy. The oysters are gritty and taste funny. "Put pepper on them," says Dad. We did and they still tasted funny. Kerry and I each get a sip of wine. It tastes like grape juice but makes your face feel warm when you swallow.

"My dad never got home before ten o'clock on Christmas Eve. They kept the barber shop open so everyone got shaved for Christmas Day. I think he always had a nip or two while they worked that night. He was very jolly when he got home." We listened as Dad retold his boyhood Christmas.

Mom gave each of us a small piece of fudge. "The rest is for tomorrow."

Now everyone retreated to the secret place where they've kept the presents hidden. Kerry and I have searched the house trying to find what Mom and Dad are getting us. We didn't find anything; either they're too clever for us or we're not getting any presents. We told each other they're clever. I took my sack down the basement into Dad's work room. All I had to wrap was the model plane I bought Kerry and a box of chocolate candy that Ida Belle Beard helped me buy for Mom and Dad. When I came back upstairs everyone was in the living room and the tree was surrounded with packages.

Kerry and I each tried a divinity pancake. Now we knew why Spot had eaten the waxed paper; the candy was stuck so tight we more or less had to chew it off. Dad said it was time to go to bed. We were ready; it had been a long day.

"I wonder what we'll get," Kerry whispered in the dark. "I want a sled."

"Me too." I didn't really want a sled; I wanted high-top shoes like most of the boys wore to school, the kind that had a little pocket just over the ankle where you could keep a pen knife. I also wanted a pen knife.

The wind slowly ebbed away during the night and the deep snow muffled every sound so we slept in dreamless sleep until long after daylight.

* * *

"Get up!" Kerry shook me awake.

The first rays of sunshine were already glittering against the frosty window and Spot was scratching at the basement door. Mom and Dad were still in bed so we let Spot outside and then headed for the living room. Our jaws dropped in amazement. Two gigantic wooden crates took up the whole room. What could they be we wondered? Beds? How could we tell our friends that we got beds for Christmas presents!

"Mom! Dad! Get up and come and see!" We ran to their bedroom. They were already pulling on robes and slippers when we got there. We ran back to the living room. "What is it?" We needed to find out what was in those two boxes. Dad was carrying a screw driver when he came out of the bedroom.

"Can you guess?" Dad pointed the screw driver at a box.

"Open it!" we cried.

"Don't you want breakfast first?"

"No! No! Please open it."

"Let's wait till after church."

Kerry grabbed one arm and I grabbed the other; we pulled Dad toward a crate. Dad smiled and started to pry one end off the first box. We crowded close hoping to get a look at what was inside.

"Turn around and close your eyes."

We turned around and closed our eyes.

"OK!"

We turned around and peered into the dark cavern and saw a wheel. BICYCLES! It was bicycles! Never in our wildest dreams would we have guessed we'd get anything as wonderful as bicycles. They weren't new; they were girl's bicycles; we didn't care, they were bicycles and they were OURS!

Our Aunts, Marge and Kay, had sent their old bicycles up from Lincoln, Nebraska by train. Dad had stored them across the street in Anderson's garage. I guess they must have had a hard time dragging those crates through the snow drifts in the middle of the night.

I got a shirt from Grandma McCauley and mittens from Grandma Dewey. Kerry gave me the same model airplane I'd given him. Mom and Dad must have noticed the Lincoln Logs - Santa gave us a set.

We had roast goose for dinner, with cranberry jelly and sweet potatoes and pumpkin pie for dessert. Mom cooked the goose liver and gave it to Spot so he wouldn't be left out. We each got another sip of wine.

The bicycles went down the basement until spring. Every now and then we'd go down there and peddle across the room, just to make sure they worked ok.

The pencil holder turned out just fine. It sat atop Mom and Dad's desk for years, now it sits on mine, the colors have faded a little and most of the red paint has worn off but it's still full of pencils.

Author's pencil holder he constructed when he was in third grade and given as a Christmas present to his parents.

Chautauqua by the Lake

Early in the summer of 1947 my mother marched both my brother and me to Chautauqua Park on Lake Okabena and enrolled us in swimming lessons. I don't remember any reluctance as we both liked the water and had spent a lot of time at the lake shore wading and playing in the shallows; so we went willingly. What could be more pleasant on a balmy morning than a jaunt to the park followed by a frolic in the water and acquiring new aquatic skills?

The morning of our first lesson we put on our bathing suits under our pants, pulled on a tee shirt, packed our towels into a cloth bag and headed down McMillan to the park without a care in the world. I don't think we noticed it but the weather was cool and there was a gentle breeze from the southwest. It's not a long walk to the park from our house; we cut over to Tenth Avenue and followed the Rock Island Railroad track to Lake Avenue and then a few short blocks and we'd arrived at the park band shell. There we were greeted by our instructors, high school girls who'd passed their lifesaving test. We doffed our shirts and pants and walked around the band shell to the swimming area. The band shell shielded us from the wind and the bright sun kept us comfortably warm. Behind the band shell was a far different story; a frigid wind shrieked around us and the sun was hidden behind the giant trees that overhang the beach. We hunched over and began to shiver, knees knocking, faces contorted. Those wonderful and kind instructors suddenly became cruel witches who forced us into the water and began their awful tortures. "Face in the water," they screamed. "Grab the dock and kick your feet," they ordered. If we rebelled, they resorted to physical abuse; taking each of us by the hand, they would show us how to perform and then force us to do the same. We soon dreaded showing up for swimming lessons. The bad news was the only technique we mastered was shivering.

That fall we moved to Mason City, Iowa and lived there for a year and a half. Mason City had a YMCA with an indoor pool. Our new friends at school there told us that we could join the Y for free and swim in that indoor pool. My brother and I went to the Y after school a few days later and asked if we could join. We may have been coached on what to say by our new friends; I don't remember. In the end a counselor gave us some paperwork for our parents to fill out and said to come back with the forms filled out and signed and we'd be able to join. We took everything home; told Mom it didn't cost anything so just sign the papers. She did as we asked without really reading any of the forms. We became members of a special YMCA group for young boys called the "Rollickys." The following spring our youth group was invited to a banquet at the Y and a newspaper photographer snapped our picture. In the next day's paper, our picture appeared under the headline "LION'S CLUB HOSTS BANQUET FOR UNDER PRIVILEGED BOYS." I don't remember the details of what followed but Mom read every word of every scrap of paper we ever brought home after that. The good news was we did become very good swimmers.

When we returned to Worthington in 1949, our new home was on West Ninth Avenue only a two block walk from Chautauqua Park. As swimmers, it was only natural that we spent much of our early teen summers at the band shell beach. There was usually a good crowd of our friends there; mostly attracted by the warm sunning area on the benches in front of the band shell. Chautauqua Park was actually a miserable place to swim.

The small beach was directly behind the band shell. There was a short, low concrete wall at the water's edge with a set of slippery stairs in the middle that led down to the water. The wall had a dock at each end which defined the swimming area. There was a floating diving platform about thirty yards from shore which was the only amenity offered. Worthington was actively dredging the lake during those years which left the water somewhat murky.

There was a life guard at the beach. Her name was Ramona. She was older; probably a college student. She was gorgeous and every boy under fifteen who swam there spent a lot of time admiring Ramona. I admired Ramona. She was friendly and I think enjoyed flirting with us; at least I believed she enjoyed flirting with me. Swimming was free but we'd have paid admission just to be close to Ramona. One day, she saved my life!

Beyond the concrete wall the shore was rock rip-rap; jagged and sharp rock. One day, a couple of us were swimming under the dock and beyond. I was swimming underwater when I hit one of those jagged rocks. It didn't really hurt and I didn't think too much of it at the time. A few moments later I hauled myself out of the water and jumped up on the dock. Girls screamed in horror and Ramona started running down the dock toward me. I was puzzled until I looked down; my whole body was covered with blood and there was a large and growing puddle of blood at my feet; it doesn't take much blood mixed with water to become a lot of blood. I'd cut open an eye lid which wasn't much of a cut but it bled quite a lot. I must have looked like I'd been attacked by the Creature from the Black Lagoon as I stood there dripping blood and covered with gore from head to foot.

The ecstasy of getting first aid from Ramona resulted in a complete mental blackout of what happened next. I do remember getting a couple of stitches at the clinic and being told not to swim for a few days. I hope I used the incident as an excuse to chat with Ramona the next time I showed up at the beach.

When we weren't swimming we were on the benches in front of the band shell. Protected from the wind and in direct sunlight those benches were a perfect place to warm up and dry off. Not only that, it was an egalitarian area where you could sit anywhere you liked and sit next to anyone you liked. It gave us the chance be friendly with girls. I suppose the reverse is true but I don't remember seeing any girls run around the end of the band shell and take a seat next to one of us. I'm positive that they did I just don't remember that they did. We learned a lot about being in close skin to skin contact with girls. One thing we learned about that was we liked it! If we were cool, I think they liked it too! I did learn that one of my classmates had webbed toes! It was all much fun but couldn't last. The older boys started showing up with Cushman scooters and motorcycles which they used to lure the girls away from those of us too young to drive. By the time I was fourteen I had a summer job at the Worthington Country Club and seldom got to swim at Chautauqua Park anymore; my only days off then were when it rained.

At the far end of the park there was a small multi-use building and a rack with several canoes. My brother and I belonged to a Scout Explorer Post which was charged with maintaining the canoes and that meant we had keys to both the building and the padlocks on the canoes. We often took advantage of the canoes and paddled all over Lake Okabena. On hot days we'd often swim across the lake using one of the canoes as a safety boat.

The summer of my sixteenth birthday two girl cousins from California, Sharane and Judai, spent a few days visiting us. One evening my brother and I took them out on Lake Okabena for a moonlight canoe ride. It was an enchanting evening; the moon was up, with no wind the lake was still as glass and the water shimmered like liquid silver in the moonlight. We drifted and watched the ripples slowly wiggle away into the silence. We stayed out on the water for a long time just drifting and talking in the tranquility of a summer night. My cousin, Judai, still talks about that night.

Beyond swimming and canoeing there were other attractions in the park. On Sundays, Howard Sevdy often brought out his Chris-Craft speed boat and gave boat rides. I'm not sure if there were any other in-board engine speed boats on the lake. The throaty roar of the speed boat's exhaust was all the advertising he needed as a crowd quickly lined up for rides whenever that sound spread over the lake.

Chasing girls wearing swimming suits was fun during our early teens but as we aged that was replaced by trolling for girls at the Wednesday night band concerts. The Worthington Community Band always packed the park, filled the benches outside the band shell and spilled over onto the grass. You had to get there early or walk a couple of blocks. We lived close so we walked those two blocks anyway. The lady who ran the popcorn wagon on Tenth Street was always at the park on band concert night and I'm sure did a brisk business during the concerts.

Much of what I saw and experienced in Worthington has faded and remains only as memories; the exception is Chautauqua Park. Everything is there almost as it was when I left. The Park superintendent's house with the little "candy store" next to the playground is gone and that awful beach was closed and replaced by the wonderful beach at Centennial Park. The Canoes are gone but the multi-purpose building is still there. You can still play checkers on the giant checkboard and toss horseshoes if you like. Crowds still fill the picnic shelter on weekends. The little World War II canon that stood guard over the picnic shelter has been removed but is being restored and will be put back on display soon I've been told. You can still show up on Wednesday night for a band concert but the popcorn wagon became too valuable and has been retired for restoration and preservation. Almost every time I return to Worthington one of my rituals is to take Crailsheim Drive around the park and admire Chautauqua Park's timeless tranquil beauty.

Band Concert at Chautauqua Park. The band shell is on the National Register of Historic Places.

Phenomena, Naturally

You climb up on the sofa, put your elbows on the back, lean out until your nose is pressed against the window and breathe out slowly. The rain spattered window is cold enough to steam up from the moisture in your breath. You wipe the foggy spot clean and see - May Baskets!

Maybe it was bad luck or maybe it's bad memory or maybe both. Either way, whenever I remember the first day in May two things come to mind – May Baskets and rain.

We manufactured our colorful harbingers of the merry month with heavy paper, cut-out flowers, crayon decorations and plenty of white paste; added a paper cupcake liner filled with peanuts, mints and chocolate kisses and we were ready. Off we'd go, trudging slowly along carrying a brown grocery sack bulging with springtime sweetness and love. When we arrived at the home of a designated recipient the sack would be opened, the chosen basket taken out and carefully placed on the step. A ring of the doorbell and we'd be off leaving the discovery of the treasure to whoever answered the door.

By the time the last delivery was made the sack was a soggy, shapeless mass, we were wet and cold and glad to be headed homeward. What I don't remember is who did we give those wonderful baskets to? Barbara Flannery? Teresa Judge? Joyce Benson? Tanya Little? Margelene Anderson? Try as I might I cannot uncover any hint. Not only does that memory elude me but I don't remember who I got baskets from either.

I might forget about May Baskets but rain I remember. Rather than the cold May Day drizzle, I delight in reliving the violent beauty and awesome power of the spring thunderstorms.

On warm soft June days the sky would blossom with towering, brilliant white cumulus clouds. The valleys and mountains of these great giants stood out so sharply against the sky that they seemed solid, like enormous scoops of Worthmore Vanilla Ice Cream. The bright sunshine, white clouds, spring green shrubbery and azure blue sky reassured us that all was well and we enjoyed gamboling in this children's paradise without a care in the world.

Maybe it was a drifting shadow or maybe a soft, distant muttering or maybe the sudden silence when the birds stopped singing; our play would stop and we'd look up. The silent giants now filled the sky, their tops still brilliant white but wreathed in a cotton candy mist, their valleys foreboding black. The serenity of the drifting cumulus had given way to a maelstrom of twisting, writhing, grotesque shapes; the sun has gone and a green glow suffuses the air with electricity and warning. Mothers call, doors slam, windows squeak shut, washing disappears and footfalls run homeward.

We'd wait by the screen door, holding it open just a crack so we could see better. Silence, no wind, no movement, only watching shapes in doorways and at windows. The bottoms of the tortured clouds sagged earthward looking as though they were holding up giant water-filled balloons. It grows steadily darker and darker.

Splat! A half-cup sized raindrop hits the sidewalk and sizzles on the hot concrete. Splat! Splat! A momentary pause and then the world disappears in a roaring cataract of rain and mist. Still no wind, we'd stand at the door breathing in the spray and watching the gutters fill with rushing water; rain barrels foaming and down spouts gushing like fire hoses.

A blue-white flash froze the raindrops in midair; one-thousand, two-thousand we counted. The house shook and rattled to the crack-bang of the thunderclap - a close one. The rain splashed our faces through the screen - it's the wind's turn now and we reluctantly closed the door and retreat to a window.

Trees turned white as their leaves, like petticoats, blew upside-down in the wind. A garbage can, orphaned by the gale, tumbled down the street like a drunken acrobat. Leaves, twigs and branches dashed madly past borne on the tempest. The house hissed and shuddered with each blast of wind. Up the street a car groped blindly along, avoiding a feint by the garbage can, headlights trying vainly to blink away the driving raindrops and windshield wipers trashing frantically at the water covered glass. A neighbor rushed bravely around the side of his house to switch the downspout into the cistern. We looked out the window, fidgeting anxiously, eager to get outside and into the action.

Then the rain slackened to a few wind-blown sheets and finally died away with the wind, leaving only dripping eaves and gurgling gutters. A soft yellow light glowed from under the retreating clouds and people emerged one by one, examining their flowers, greeting each other and smiling with relief. We ran barefoot outdoors into the street and jumped into the disappearing rivers.

Afternoon storms were exciting and fun, not so with the monsters of the night.

The curtains hang slack and still in the airless open windows. Quiet, not even dogs bark in the black heat. We lay in bed wearing only undershorts and half covered by a sheet, sweating and sticking in the hot, damp dark.

My brother, Kerry, and I slept in the same bed and hot nights together meant shifting and thrashing and sheet pulling and getting up for another drink of water and the hope of a cooling breeze. We'd look out the window over the kitchen sink and watch the flicker of the heat lightning to the north. Then back to bed to toss and shift and turn and pull and finally fitful sleep.

How does the night storm creep up unnoticed? We'd wake up to the sound of pouring rain and booming thunder, our bedroom flickering with blue lightning flashes. The curtains whipping in the wind, water slashing through the open screens and spraying the room. Jumping up, we'd rush to close windows and doors and then stand dripping, naked, hot and breathless as the wind and rain roared all around us in the darkness. After what seemed like hours the storm would pass and we'd reopen windows, shuffle back to bed damper and hotter and angry because we knew that our baseball gloves were soaking wet on the back steps.

We were asleep when Mom came into our room at the start of one of those storms just as a bolt of lightning burned a hole through our bedroom window screen. As she watched, a blue ball of electricity raced around the room burning a black path to a light switch which melted in an explosion of sparks. That was too close!

After a storm the Street Department often had to clean debris from the streets. A tank truck with spray nozzles on the front would drive slowly along and wash the litter into the gutters. Then a crew of men would appear, armed with long handled square shovels and, following a flatbed truck, they would rhythmically shovel the gutters clean, tossing waste onto the truck. When they came to a catch basin, its grate would be lifted and long handled dippers would be extracted from the truck. We would crowd around and pear into the black watery depths as the muck was dipped out. Following the street crew was almost as much fun as wading in the rain rivers.

It rained in the fall of 1949. It rained for days and days, a steady, dreary, slow, drizzling, muddy rain. Nothing dried; no farm field-work could get done. Fall squished slowly toward winter and everyone watched the sky, hoping vainly for sun and drying weather.

We stayed indoors, read comic books, played Monopoly, listened to music on the radio and drove our parents crazy.

In October a storm with hurricane winds blasted the soaked farmland and the soggy cornstalks, already weakened by a heavy infestation of corn borers, broke and fell flat. Whole fields were leveled as though cut down by a giant scythe. The damage was so bad and the storm so spectacular that Worthington even made Ripley's "Believe It Or Not" - the movie playing at the Gay Drive-in Theater was "Slattery's Hurricane" and the coming attraction was (you guessed it) "Gone With The Wind."

Mechanical corn pickers were mostly useless in wet fields full of flattened corn stalks so we got out of school to help pick corn by hand. We walked the fields and picked up ears missed by the machines.

The farm that Kerry and I picked on still had horses and we got to pick with them. When the farmer drove us to the field he said just pick the ears (he showed us how to twist them off the stalk but we didn't have to husk them), throw them in the wagon and be careful not to miss any. We asked what we should do about the horses and he told us that they knew how to pick corn and would know where to go and what to do. They did too; when we got to the front of the wagon they would pull ahead a short distance and stop, when we got to the end of the field they would go over four rows and turn the other way.

We picked corn that way for about a week and it was wet and damp that whole week too.

Nature's show wasn't always stormy or disastrous; in fact we were witness to an event both beautiful and rare - one that I thought I'd most likely never see again - a total eclipse of the sun.

Early on the morning of June 30, 1954 all our family got up and drove out to the Worthington airport. A large crowd was already on hand, waiting silently in the cool morning air. The eclipse began shortly after sunrise so the airport with its clear view of the eastern horizon was an ideal spot. We were equipped with exposed film negatives and sheets of cardboard with pinholes for making a "camera obscura" used to project the image of the sun on a sheet of white paper.

There was no daylight saving time then so sunup was very early, about 5:00 AM. When we arrived at the airport, around 6:00 AM, the sun was already partially covered by the moon. The effect of the diminishing sunlight is gradual and not at all like twilight or sunset. The light softened gradually and distant objects slowly faded, eventually becoming indistinct and finally disappearing, as though a veil of gauze was being drawn over the landscape. The sky darkened from blue to violet to purple and the stars began to appear as more and more of the sun was covered. In the dwindling daylight the birds began singing their evening songs and the crowd stirred with anticipation.

The sky became deep purple and the remaining slender sliver of the sun began to fade so fast we could see it slide behind the moon until only "Bailey's Beads" remained. One by one these shafts of sunlight shining between the gaps in the mountains on the moon winked out until the last "bead" vanished and the sun was gone. The fiery white halo of the sun's corona surrounded the black disc of the moon, the birds stopped singing and silence enveloped us.

The semi-darkness cast an enchanting spell; everyone took on a ghostly appearance in the corona's dim glow. The gazing crowd stood still, not talking except for soft gasps of awe, hardly breathing, transfixed as our distant ancestors must have been, knowing full well that light would reappear but unable to escape the nagging fear that maybe it wouldn't.

The totality of an eclipse lasts only a few minutes — three is about the maximum. Worthington was not exactly in the center of the shadow's path so the sun was covered for only about two minutes.

When the first bright flash of light appeared at the top of the moon, the "diamond ring", everyone exhaled, the birds chirped and the tension was broken. How quickly the light returned. The covering had seemed to go so slowly and now the moon just slid quickly away and the light increased in intensity with each second. Their faith restored, the crowd quickly drifted away, probably discovering an appetite suppressed by the primeval anxiety they had just experienced.

It was still early when we got home so I rode my bicycle over to Chautauqua Park for lack of anything better to do. The park was teaming with warblers. I've never seen so many birds and such variety - masked Wilson's, grey and yellow Myrtle, orange and black Redstart, and Yellow warblers. As they darted quickly from place to place they made the park twinkle with bright colors. Nature can sure put on a colorful show.

Fortunately, I've been given another chance to witness this unusual event a second time. On August 21, 2017, my son Patrick and I drove to Geneva, Nebraska to observe the solar eclipse. The weather seemed intent on frustrating our efforts as clouds obscured the sun for much of the time leading up to totality. With the sun already largely covered by the moon, the clouds suddenly slid away and we were able to view this astronomical majesty under clear skies and I was able to again marvel at the beautiful spectacle.

Trick or Treat or the Rack

It's not that we were any better behaved than other kids our age, I think it was more a matter of not being able to do anything bad enough to warrant close contact with officers of the law. As we grew older that changed from time to time but I still have only vague recollections of policemen when I was young. One exception was on Halloween.

We were involved in the normal activities of that day, sacks in hand we set off at sunset and trick-n-treated our way to a collection of apples, oranges, home-made popcorn balls, peanut brittle, banana flavored marshmallow candies (yech) and candy kisses. Once in a while a real treat, the Catholic Sisters always gave out Hersey bars and a few less imaginative households gave us a nickel. To those we felt had slighted us or otherwise deserved ill treatment - a swipe of soap on a window.

Listening to the older boys as they told of wondrous feats of Halloween engineering and daring-do - putting buggies atop water towers, pump organ on a front porch, tipping outdoor toilets - made us wish that there were still buggies, pump organs and outdoor toilets available.

We did, however, dream of achieving a notorious reputation in this regard and from time-to-time experimented.

After trick-n-treating was exhausted we'd head downtown to the State Theater for a night of horror movies; sponsored by some civic organization trying desperately and fruitlessly to keep us occupied and off the streets until bed time. My ears still throb whenever I think of Halloween night at the State Theater. The crowded theater was more of a riot that anything else. Anyway, going to the show gave us the opportunity to display our evil ingenuity.

On cool autumn nights sparrows sought shelter in the evergreen bushes growing close to the houses. As we walked toward downtown on Halloween we'd check likely bushes for sleeping sparrows. When one was spotted we'd creep into action. Slowly, slowly a hand would slide into the bush, fingers cautiously surrounding the oblivious prey and then NAB! Most of the time we missed but after several tries a couple of birds would be safely tucked into a jacket pocket. The warm, dark pocket would calm the birds down and soon they were again fast asleep.

Once seated in the screaming, jumping, running, throwing, brawling theater, we'd be patient for the proper moment. When the pandemonium flagged for just an instant, a bird would be gently taken out of its pocket and tossed skyward! The confused sparrow would zoom and career over the heads of the cheering savages much to our delight, at last landing on one of the great art-deco lights along the walls. By the end of the night each light had its own sparrow. I'll bet Gay Hower and his theater staff hated Halloween and the job of chasing those sparrows out the next day.

My brother, Kerry, and one of his friends were headed homeward down Tenth Street after the Halloween movie when they discovered an opportunity setting right there in front of Ahlf's Drug Store - a bicycle rack. Now I should mention that this was before the days of "hi-tech", so the rack was made of wood - sturdily made with two-by-fours and bolts and frequently painted with layer after layer of dark green paint. The boys eagerly grabbed the rack and began to drag it into position like a barricade across Tenth Street. So intent were they on their act of daring-do that they failed to see a policeman walking up the street.

"You're under arrest," he announced with authority. "You'll have to come down to the station and bring that bicycle rack along as evidence."

Their bravado gone, the now quivering penitents hoisted the evidence and gloomily followed the officer across the street, past the County Court House and over to City Hall. There they set the Bicycle rack down and were ushered into the brightly lit Police Station.

The arresting office explained to the Sergeant in lurid detail how he'd come upon these two incorrigible juvenile delinquents and caught them red handed endangering the life and limb of every law abiding citizen. The Sergeant nodded knowingly and the boys now expected the worst.

The Sergeant speculated. "I suppose we should lock them up, call their parents and hold them for court in the morning."

Two hearts sank and two faces turned white with terror. It was bad enough being locked up and possibly facing life in jail but how could they face their parents? The shame would be too much.

"I don't know Sarge. We've never had any trouble with these two before and they look like we could take a chance on them going straight. What do you think?"

The Sergeant pondered, frowning at the two quivering lumps of gelatin. "Do you two think we should give you another chance?"

Both boys nodded enthusiastically.

"Ok, you can go this time, but if we ever see either of you again there'll be big trouble."

With relief, they turned and started out the door.

"Be sure and put that bike rack back in front of Ahlf's where it belongs. Remember, we'll be keeping an eye on both of you."

They hoisted the rack and began the trek back to the drug store. In the terror of their arrest they'd carried the rack all the way to the Police Station without noticing how heavy it was; now with each step their arms ached and the muscles in their backs burned. They dragged, pushed, slid, staggered and strained their way the two blocks back to the drug store. There, chastened, sore and exhausted they dropped the sturdy bicycle rack and limped slowly homeward.

There's something to be said for the psychology of the small town police. They may not be well equipped to solve baffling murder mysteries or outwit clever international jewel thieves but at protecting small boys from themselves they have no equals.

High Noon

The sun is bright, the sky is brilliantly blue and the air is cool and crisp; a fall morning as glorious as any we've ever seen. Saturday mornings on Tenth Street are always busy but on the Saturday of the opening day of pheasant hunting season the street is crowded with men and women clad in plaid shirts, canvas pants and hunting vests; many carrying cased shotguns. The pheasant population around Worthington exploded after the end of the war and by 1951 many Twin City hunters were drawn to the Worthington area confident of success. The bright sunshine and crisp fall air combined with the crowd of hunters colorfully clad in hunting garb create an almost carnival atmosphere. The mood is electric with anticipation as they jostle each other, sweeping from restaurants and cafes out to their cars or greeting each other on the sidewalk and boisterously exchanging plans for the upcoming hunt. Bird dogs tug at leashes and bark in their eagerness to get into the field. Soon the throng can no longer be contained and everyone rushes to their cars and streams into the countryside where they cluster in farmyards and prepare for the hunt.

My older brother, Kerry, works at O. P. Skaggs grocery and works on Saturdays; even on opening day. That's bad for him but an opportunity for me; Kerry has a shotgun and I don't. Kerry is working which means I can borrow his shotgun! I've forgotten what this favor cost but he did indeed lend me the gun for that day. Now all I had to do was to convince Mom that I could venture out on my own with a shotgun. Somehow I convinced her that a thirteen year-old wouldn't shoot anything other than pheasants and not shoot himself! There was one last hurdle, getting to a place to hunt. Dad was out of town with Eddie Skeets' orchestra so Mom would have to drive me somewhere to hunt. I'm sure there was a price to pay for these favors but it couldn't have been too bad because I have no recollection of her demands.

I got up early on opening day and put on my hunting outfit, a long sleeved shirt, jeans, boots and a light jacket, and headed downtown to buy a box of shotgun shells. I worked my way through the crowd, heading for Rickbeil's Hardware. I quickly selected a box of 16 gauge shells and proudly set them on the counter in front of the clerk and handed him some of my hard-earned paper route money. Shells in hand I headed homeward.

Mom drove me to a spot a couple of miles south of town toward Lake Ocheda on the road leading to Hawkinson Bridge. We stopped at a corner where a narrow township road headed east skirting the north shore of the lake. Kerry and I had gone out there before where we practiced shooting his shotgun over a slough along the lake shore. As I unloaded my stuff out of the car, Mom and I agreed that she'd meet me at 3 o'clock back at this spot. I stepped away from the car as Mom turned it around and then I watched her drive off back toward town. It wasn't noon yet so I sat down along the edge of the road to wait.

The open country is usually quiet in the fall, meadowlarks seldom sing, redwing blackbirds and goldfinches are done nesting so we don't see much of them. I watched as a sparrow hawk (American Kestrel) hovered over a spot down the road ditch and then swooped down to snatch a grass hopper. I brought my Minneapolis Star Journal newspaper bag along to carry my gear – shotgun shells, canteen and a couple of candy bars. I reached into the bag, brought out my canteen and took a drink of water. As I was screwing the cap back on the canteen I heard the toot of the noon whistle from the power plant; the hunt was on!

I unsheathed the shotgun, stuffed the cloth sheath into the newspaper bag, took out the box of shells, loaded the gun, slung the bag over my shoulder and stepped downward into the grassy bottom of the roadside ditch. The weeds and grass were only a foot or so high so walking wasn't difficult. Cradling the gun I strode forward excited but mentally unprepared.

I had only taken a few steps before a cock pheasant burst upward out of the weeds squawking and beating its wings furiously. I fumbled, pushed off the safety, swung the gun to my shoulder and fired. I may have closed my eyes as I shot because I didn't actually see the bird until it tumbled toward the ground. Somehow I'd managed to actually shoot it! I could see where it landed so I started to walk quickly toward the spot. Before I'd take more than a dozen steps another pheasant erupted from the weeds. Luckily I'd ejected the spent cartridge and reloaded after my first shot so I was rewarded with a bang when I pulled the trigger on the second bird. This time I saw the pheasant collapse and fall. I picked up the first bird, dropped it into my bag and headed to where I saw the second bird fall. I found it easily and dropped it into the bag.

I was elated! Two birds already in the bag; I'd never imagined that kind of success. My brother and I and a couple of our friends went hunting whenever we could but it usually meant walking so we couldn't go very far from town unless Mom or Dad drove us. Rabbits and squirrels were the standard fare. My dad had a Remington Model 34 .22 rifle that we shared.

Sometimes, if there was a friend along everyone had a gun. So, we knew how to hunt and we'd both had gun safety training so we understood how to handle guns safely. We were serious and didn't fool around when we were carrying loaded guns. I'd never actually shot anything with a shotgun before so actually hitting two pheasants was probably beginners luck more that natural skill.

I continued walking slowly up the road ditch. This time I saw the bird as it ran forward through the weeds for a few feet before launching itself into the air. I lifted the gun, punched the safety off and fired. The bird fell on the road. The daily bag limit in 1951 was three cock pheasants and I now had my limit. After picking the bird and stuffing it in my bag I looked at my watch; it was only twenty minutes after twelve! I turned around and looked back toward where I'd started; the main road was less than fifty yards away.

There was one shell left in the gun. I ejected it and dropped it into the bag and pulled out the sheath and slid the gun into it and tied it shut. I was done for the day and Mom wouldn't be back to pick me up for another two and half hours. I pondered that for a few minutes and then decided to start walking home. It wouldn't be too arduous to walk the four miles home and I'd be there long before Mom would leave to come and pick me up.

The walk was a pleasant and somewhat triumphal. Here I was marching along carrying a shotgun and a bag full of pheasants for everyone to see; surely they would infer great hunting skill and nod knowingly as they passed. Memory is a tricky thing and I don't remember seeing a single soul as I plodded along, not on the gravel road, not as I went through the railroad underpass along Lake Okabena, not as I walked down Lake Street and Lake Avenue. I arrived home completely unnoticed.

Mom was relieved to see me and pleased to see the three pheasants I pulled from the paperboy's bag. Triumph didn't overcome the household rule – you shot it or caught it and you got to clean it. Luckily, I'd never cleaned a pheasant before so Mom said she'd help. Cleaning pheasants is pretty simple, slit the skin up the breast, cut off the head, wings and feet, pull the skin off and scoop out the body cavity and you're done.

"Let's be sure to pick out the BB's." Mom picked up a carcass and began to look closely at the back then turned it over and examined the breast. She shook her head, dropped the bird and picked up a second one repeating the examination.

I'd been checking the remaining bird and didn't spot any BB holes either. We were both puzzled by the lack of pellet wounds anywhere. Mom pawed through the pile of discarded skin and feathers and extracted a head which she examined closely and then turned to me with a smile.

"There's a single pellet in the very top of the head."

She showed me the spot.

"I'll bet you did the same thing with the other two. You shot high enough that only one or two pellets hit them in the head. You were lucky."

So it was beginner's luck after all. However, we still enjoyed a wonderful Sunday dinner of fried pheasant in cream sauce.

The lucky first-time hunter proudly displays his birds.

Drive'm Crazy

When we moved back to Worthington from Mason City, Iowa in 1949, the time had come when we could no longer get along without a car. The next spring Dad brought home a black, 1939 Pontiac two-door. Good used cars where still scarce yet, even though it had been five years since the end of World War II; that is unless you bought a new one and it would be a long time before anyone in our family even thought of a new car. The black Pontiac would have to do. It was a sturdy, work-horse type of car, not sleek, bullet shaped like the new Studebakers, not V8 modern like the new Fords and not hansom, fast-backed like the new Chevrolets; it was just a somewhat overweight looking, plain, solid car - but a car nonetheless. Dad didn't have a Minnesota Driver's License so he had to go downtown and take both the written and behind the wheel test. For several evenings he drove around the neighborhood practicing and I even talked him into letting me ride along. I had to promise to keep quiet and not ask questions so he could concentrate on proper technique. He passed the tests easily and a short time later Mom did too. We were part of the American Automobile Dream; we could go anywhere we wanted, rain or shine.

Kerry and I both pestered to learn to drive. You could get a license at fifteen then and we wanted to be ready. Kerry must have been fourteen and I was thirteen when our constant lobbying paid off. Dad took us out to the driveway and our lessons began. We were lucky to have Dad for a teacher, his musical training gave him the exact outlook he needed to make our learning proceed easily and successfully - learn the fundamentals and advance one step at a time with patience and repetition.

First we were taught the proper starting technique - put key in ignition, turn on ignition, pull out choke knob, push in clutch with left foot, push down starter pedal with toe of right foot while pushing on gas pedal with heel of right foot - this may seem simple but to a nervous, thirteen year old that was a bewildering number of tasks to both remember and execute all at once. We started, raced the engine, ground the starter, raced the engine, traded places and continued to abuse the poor old Pontiac. At last we could get behind the wheel and start the engine smoothly. We were even allowed to start the car before we went to church or to the store. After the engine was running, we'd slide over and Mom or Dad would take control.

Then one day Dad announced we were ready for phase two - low gear. When starting the car we were taught to find neutral (this car had a manual transmission as did all our cars until I left home), center the shift lever and let the clutch out slowly just to make sure. Yes, we're in neutral. Ok, push in the clutch, pull the lever toward yourself and pull it down. That's low gear! Now let out the clutch slooowly while you push down gently on the gas pedal.

Our driveway went alongside the house and after it ended there was a large garden without any breakable objects close by so any runaway wouldn't be too bad. I think Dad must have kept his hand on the ignition key anyway, just in case. Once we got rolling we let up on the gas, pushed in the clutch and put on the brakes.

Now I hope you appreciate how many different multi-part procedures we've already had to learn and we're just to low gear! We didn't have any trouble doing all of them but we didn't always get the sequence right. We lurched, stalled, raced and jerked. When the car was brought to a successful stop we shifted to reverse - find neutral, pull shift lever toward you and push up. We then tried to back up with results similar to those we achieved going forward. As with our previous lessons we were soon able to start the car, go forward in low gear and backward in reverse.

One lovely Sunday afternoon Dad asked if we thought we were ready for the big time - second gear! We nodded eagerly but inside Kerry and I were both filled with dread. This lesson was beyond the confining limits of our driveway; we headed out to the edge of town, by the cemetery on the road that leads to Fauskee's Grade on Lake Ocheda. The gravel road was wide, straight and, best of all, mostly deserted on Sunday afternoon.

You got behind the wheel, palms slippery with sweat, stomach in knots, trying to look calm. Go through the starting procedure and you're ready. Somehow the car seems to have gotten bigger; you can barely see over the dashboard, the wheel seems enormous - too big to turn and the road is so narrow. Wait, here comes a car! You exhale and gulp another breath.

Now it begins. Let out the clutch, press down on the gas - whoops forgot to shift into low! Begin again, let out the clutch and give it some gas. Joy! We're rolling. Now quickly, let up on the gas, push in clutch, push up on shift lever to neutral, push shift lever away from you and up into second, let out clutch, push down on gas! How will we ever master it? But it's too late; we've made second gear and are gaining speed. Oh, oh! Steer!

We have to steer! Panic! The car seems to have a mind of its own. Push in clutch, let up on gas pedal and put on brakes. Stop and go limp.

I wonder sometimes how we ever were able to master the intricate processes required and to do everything simultaneously. But we did. After several turns at second gear we moved up into high but that was no big deal, the terror of second and the open road had been conquered. We learned to steer, turn corners, and stop at stop signs. The only maneuver left was parallel parking. We knew that you couldn't pass the driving test unless you could parallel park. Well, we were too young to take the test anyway so why worry about little things like parallel parking. We got to drive home from church or drive to school. Actually we didn't drive all the way - just a few blocks from our house or the last few blocks to our house. We weren't ready for traffic.

Brad Dickey had a 1947 Chevy Fleetline, dark blue, lowered, fender skirts, shaved hood and custom grille. He and I were friends so I helped him work on that beautiful machine. He ordered a dual exhaust system from the J C Whitney mail order catalog and I helped him install it. When the job was finished we got in the car and started out around Lake Okabena to see how the new mufflers sounded - the ideal was a deep rumble, loud but legal. As we approached Ludlow's,

Brad stopped and said he was getting in the trunk to get the real sound of those mufflers and I was going to drive. Me! Drive! I'd never driven "solo" before. I didn't have a license. What if the police saw me? What if there was an accident?

Brad was older and I couldn't tell him I wasn't ready; so I acted nonchalant and slid over to the driver's seat. Brad got in the trunk and hollered for me to get going. Luckily I didn't kill the engine or start off with a jerk.

The road curves gently around the lake but I felt as if I was driving in the Alps! Even twenty-five miles an hour seemed like Memorial Day at the Indianapolis 500! Then I came upon two boys on bicycles and there was a car coming from the other direction! If I pulled off the road I would have driven into Vance's living room! I would have to make it between the bicyclists and the car without killing anyone. I did it.

I finally stopped at Slater Park and got out, trying to look as if I enjoyed the drive. I had to lean against the car because my knees were shaking so bad I couldn't stand up. If Brad noticed he didn't say anything. After that episode driving was not quite so stressful.

My first car was a 1931 Ford Model A Coupe. I drove it home from Brookings, South Dakota. The engine was very fickle and ran only when it felt like it. I got as far as Rushmore once and had to be towed home by Art Riss and his red, 1937 Chevy. After that the Model A was mostly a driveway queen.

I'm sure that what Mom and Dad remember about that car is a crowd of teenage boys, leaning under the hood or lying under the front end, like a college of surgeons performing a delicate open heart operation. We'd tinker with it, get it running, drive around town until it quit running and then push it home. I was probably lucky that it ran so seldom, the mechanical brakes made stopping very tricky, dangerous and lengthy. In the fall I forgot to drain the water out of the engine block, it froze and cracked the cylinder head. The Model A was done for and I sold it to a farmer who made a trailer out of the rear end and junked the rest.

Author on left with Brad Dickey and friends working on getting the Model A running.

Let there be Light

On a lovely spring day in the early 1950s, the Worthington merchants held a sidewalk sale and everyone in town headed downtown to look for bargains. My brother Kerry and a few of his friends stopped at Ricker's Photography Studio on Third Avenue. Ricker's had a variety of photo supplies and equipment on sale. As the boys fingered cameras, lenses and film, a strange object caught my brother's eye; it was a very, very large flashbulb and it had a screw-in base just like a regular light bulb. It was on sale for fifty cents, a price too low for my brother to resist so he bought it.

Like most treasures which have no practical use, Kerry brought the giant flashbulb home and added to the other treasures in his junk box at the back of the closet where it sat, largely forgotten until later that fall.

We had finished eating supper and were headed outside to play in the gathering twilight when a sudden brain wave caused Kerry to reverse course, go to the closet junk box, retrieve to flashbulb and wait for mother to leave the kitchen. As soon as she was away, he quickly unscrewed the lightbulb from a wall lamp by the kitchen cupboards that mom usually tuned on whenever she did the supper dishes. Kerry screwed in the flashbulb and then rejoined us outside.

My mother was a creature of habit and Kerry had noticed that as she prepared to clear the table after supper, she first turned on that wall light. As she always did, she bent over and looked directly at the bulb and then switched the lamp on; no one knows why, but she always looked directly at the bulb when she turned the switch.

Whatever game we were playing in the front yard was suddenly illuminated by a flash of brilliant light; a flash so bright that we swore afterward that we could see light in the cracks of the siding on the house. It seemed like the whole neighborhood lit up.

Not wanting to give himself away, Kerry waited for a minute or so before strolling casually into the house and walking into the kitchen. Mother was busily doing the dishes and didn't even turn around at the sound of Kerry.

"Grab a towel and start wiping," was all she said.

Kerry was crushed. Not a peep about the flash. Not a single reference to his daring and mischievous act. They finished the dishes in silence and Mom simply went out into the living room and turned on the radio.

Many years after we'd all grown up and left home we returned for one of our usual boisterous family gatherings and the flashbulb incident somehow came up. Mother delightedly recounted her experience.

"I reached up and turned on the light and was completely blinded by the bright flash. I don't know why but I realized that one of my two oldest sons had set me up and I was determined not to give the culprit the satisfaction of any response. I was totally blind! I had to feel my way over to the sink and carefully feel for the dishes. I knew the first one in would be the guilty party but I wouldn't let on. By the time we were done washing dishes I could see just enough to walk to the living room and find the radio."

Sometimes our pranks worked but usually our parents outsmarted us.

The Red Menace

In the early 1950s Americans were terrified by the thought of a Soviet sneak attack. People started building bomb shelters in their back yards and stockpiling food and water in their basements. Soon the military planners became obsessed with the notion of "Early Warning." Our Airforce started building air bases in the northern Artic and design work was begun on a distant early warning radar network, dubbed "The DEW Line," that would span the upper Artic from Alaska to Greenland; giving us the capability to spot Communist airplanes long before they reached our borders. But completion of those airbases and radar networks was years away and we needed something NOW!

The Airforce planners hit upon a simple and relatively cheap stopgap system; recruit volunteer spotters and spread them across the U.S. in a network of observation posts, manned twenty-four hours a day and connected via telephone to a central headquarters with direct communication to Strategic Air Command bases where fighters and bombers stood ready to launch. Worthington joined this new Ground Observer Corps system (GOC) in 1952 with the construction of an observation post atop the YMCA. The now demolished YMCA building had originally been constructed as an opera house with the rear of the building elevated to house the mechanism for handing stage scenery. That higher roof area provided an ideal 360 degree view of the horizon, ideal for spotting incoming Communist bombers! A small room, no more than ten feet by ten feet with wide windows all around was quickly constructed. A small round plotting table sat in the middle, covered with a compass rose and a swiveling pointer so the observers could pinpoint the exact compass position of any aircraft they sighted. A telephone, binoculars and two chairs completed the furnishings. I don't remember for sure but I think they had to construct an outside stairway to get up to that high roof. Anyway, inside or out, it was a long climb to get up there.

My brother Kerry, classmates Dave Johnson, Bob Tachovsky, LeRoy Nau and I were among many who volunteered to man this outpost. There was intense training in aircraft identification which even included a series of fly-bys where we were gathered at the old Nobles County Fair Grounds on Clary Street, seated in the grandstand bleachers and were asked to identify several World War II fighters and bombers as they whizzed by in front of us. As young boys, fascinated by aviation, we had no trouble naming the various planes and always got high marks. After our training was completed we were given a pair of "GOC" wings to pin on our jackets and assigned shifts (mostly at night as we had school during the day) in the high rooftop post.

Out location was identified by a "call sign." Ours was "Kilo Papa two three Black." When we manned the post we called the communication center at specified intervals, "This is Kilo Papa two three Black, reporting in. No activity to report." Once in a great while we'd spot the lights of an airplane and quickly swing the compass pointer to determine its direction from our post. Then we'd pick up the phone and report, "Kilo Papa two three Black observing an unidentified aircraft at two hundred thirty degrees south bound." Sometimes the plane was a test to see if we were paying attention. Mostly we just spent four hours scanning the dark skies with our binoculars and talking with each other.

It wasn't long before the Airforce built a radar base on the Buffalo Ridge just south of Chandler, Minnesota, and the Worthington GOC post was shut down and we were no longer needed.

While Worthington was no longer directly involved with the Airforce in protection measures, Heron Lake was. As electronic systems became more sophisticated and air-to-air missiles became powerful defensive tools, we needed to test our capabilities against the Communists. Heron Lake was designated a "Soviet Radar and Missile Training Site." Soon railroad cars arrived, loaded with radar and radio antennas and crowded with windowless boxes where technicians could simulate everything we thought the Soviets could do to shoot down our bombers and fighters when we attacked them.

For several weeks in the summer of 1954 or 55, we would see a variety of bombers and fighters, some high in the sky but most very, very low as they swooped over the countryside "attacking" Heron Lake. The giant B36 Peacemaker with six big radial engines and four jet engines was the most majestic. The Peacemaker was so large it appeared to be gliding leisurely through the air. If the giant B36 was close enough, the engine noise was awesome. We also looked in awe at the sleek and deadly B47 Stratojet bombers that slashed through the sky with a loud roar and a trail of sooty smoke. If we were outside we'd stop whatever we were doing and watch the deadly airshow; half expecting to hear bombs exploding at Heron Lake. I often wondered what it must have been like in Heron Lake when they were "attacked" by the Air Force. With the radar warning system complete and newer threats elsewhere in the world Worthington finally seemed far away from sneak attack.

Decades after the old high school building was demolished, a project was started to clean out the basement of the Memorial Auditorium which was used as gym locker rooms for the now gone high school and had sat untouched since. A classmate of mine reported that a cache of boxes filled with Civil Defense food and water was discovered in a small storeroom in auditorium basement. The basement had once been designated a fallout shelter during the early 1950s.

Stage Fright

I've written little about my high school experiences — mostly too boring to recount and likely of little interest to readers as well. One school activity that is unique enough to recount was my participation in the 1955 Junior Class Play. Our play, "The Vampire Bat," was a forgettable murder mystery which tells you I've forgotten the plot and almost all of the story as well. What I do remember is that we had a cast that performed well and the play was a general success with a couple of notable exceptions.

There was a scene late in the play where Beverly Smail's character confronted the villain, played by Ted Ludlow. Beverly was armed with a real revolver loaded with blanks and her character was supposed to shoot the villain. I don't think Beverly had ever handled a revolver before and I'm not sure she was carefully instructed on how far away she should stay from Ted and that she should point the barrel behind Ted and not straight at him. During a rehearsal the time came for

Beverly to fire the gun for the first time. The director called for action, Beverly confronted Ted, whipped out the pistol and at close range, fired the gun. Ted yowled in pain and clutched his side. Beverly was so close that many small particles of paper and powder residue pierced Ted's costume and peppered his skin. Luckily Beverly was still far enough away to cause only superficial injury. After that, the scene was reenacted with more emphasis on where to stand and where to point the pistol and Ted survived without further injury.

One of the characters in the play was a black servant. Worthington in 1955 wasn't a diverse community; our only non-Caucasian was a man named Wong who ran the laundry across Ninth Street from the Armory. With no black students, someone had to be transformed into a black servant; as it turned out, I was the one designated to undergo that miracle of makeup. Changing my face and hands from light to dark was easy, just smear on colored cream makeup. My facial features where transformed by using makeup putty to broaden my nose. The result was a somewhat grotesque looking blue-eyed parody of a black servant. The bigger problem was how to change my lovely, wavy red hair into a black, kinky African hairdo; my mother came to the rescue with the aid of her friend, Donna Simpson. Donna was a beautician who worked in Phil Fiola's Barber and Beauty Salon in the basement below the Band Box Cleaners on Tenth Street. The two concocted a two-step plan. The day before our first performance, Mom and I went over to Simpson's house and started my kitchen makeover. First they gave me a "permanent wave," to put my hair up in tight curls that would make it sort of kinky. As I recall the permanent wave chemistry at time was pretty harsh and very hard on your hair. Once my hair was set, they launched into the next step; changing the color from red to black. The chemistry chosen for this procedure was a "black rinse;" a dye that was guaranteed to wash out once the play was over. I was assured that after the final performance of the play all I had to do was wash my hair and the red would return. Of course, there would be a few weeks of tight curly hair but a haircut would remove most of the curls and I'd be back to normal.

The performances of the play went off without a hitch. Beverly's position and aim were flawless and the villain was killed but Ted survived unscathed. No one complained about the performance of the black servant and I even rated a picture in the 1955 WHS Trojan Yearbook. The cast party after the final performance was a blast. We were pleased.

The next day, the school debate team departed for Northfield to participate in the Shattuck Invitational Debate Tournament. I was on the team and was looking forward to the trip. The 1954 team was a powerhouse led by Gary Crippen and Burdell Doe. Both had graduated so we were rebuilding but prospects looked good. Shattuck is a classy private boarding school and we'd be well taken care of there.

Without a care in the world, I came home from the cast party, took a shower and washed my hair. I finished my shower, toweled off and looked in the mirror and recoiled in horror! My hair wasn't its old color, it was no longer black, and it was PURPLE! Here I was headed for a sophisticated educational institution, representing our school before a panel of judges in a series of public debates with purple hair. Panic doesn't begin to describe my emotional state! I was supposed to be an intellectual capable of deep thought and logical argument and I looked like a purple headed freak. I don't remember any of my team members making fun of me on the trip to Northfield where Shattuck School is located. I may have worn a cap as a cover up. Maybe they just avoided looking at me. The worst was yet to come.

The Worthington High School Debate team participated in about eleven tournaments during the winter and spring so we got to know many of the teams from the other schools around Minnesota. At Shattuck, all of the participating teams were invited to a mixer scheduled the evening before the tournament began. We enjoyed meeting many of the debaters from other schools and looked forward socializing. The mixer was held that evening in an elegant hall with dark paneling, book lined walls and columns supporting an overhead walkway. I spent most of the evening lurking in the shadows of the columns hoping no one would notice my purple hairdo. My memory of the tournament was blanked out by a "purple fog" and no trace of the event remains in my brain except lurking in the shadows hoping no one would see my purple hair. I had Phil Fiola give me a short hair cut on Monday after school so the curls and most of the purple disappeared.

My thespian ardor was pretty much squashed by my experience in the Junior Class Play. I did get on stage once more a few years ago when I did a walk-on costumed as a Russian orthodox priest for a performance in "Fiddler on the Roof." I wore a religious head piece so my hair didn't get into the act.

After the Pavement ends

Although we always lived in town, I was fascinated by farm country. We didn't have a car but from time to time were invited along to ride to a nearby town which meant watching the rural countryside pass by as we drove along. Even today as I drive around the farmland near Worthington I get great satisfaction from viewing the bucolic countryside and am pleased to be able to see all the way to the horizon, a treat not readily available to those who now dwell in larger metropolitan areas. Can I not help but treat you to a few memories of my early contact with rural Nobles County?

In February, 1944, my youngest brother, Jamie, died of whooping cough; he was only eleven months old. My mother was doubly devastated; she'd not only lost Jamie but he had become a truly captivating baby and Mom loved him dearly. In the days following Jamie's death, the presence of my brother, Kerry, and I only exacerbated her anguish. A family friend, Audrey

James, offered to take Kerry and I for a few days to help Mom and Dad recover from their sorrow.

Audrey taught school in a one-room country school house near Slayton, Minnesota. I don't have a clear memory of where we stayed but I think Audrey lived on a farm near the school. My brother and I easily fit into that school and it soon felt like we'd always been part of that mixture of kids. We recited, practiced reading and writing, did arithmetic using flash cards and stood in line for spelling bees. I think we were there for two weeks. Audrey James went on to become Superintendent of Murray County Schools and remained a close friend of our family.

* * *

In the summer of 1953 Bruce Heyl was the first of my friends to get a car and suddenly there was a world of opportunity. None of us had been selected for jobs detasseling corn and all of the other summer jobs were taken so we were eager to find something that earned us some money. Someone suggested shocking oats. Farmers who still threshed oats, rather than combining, needed to cut the ripe oats and bundle them. The small bundles were collected and placed in a uniform stack called a "shock." Shocks helped keep the grain dry until the shocks were loaded onto a bundle wagon and hauled to the threshing machine. Stacking bundles into shocks was done by hand and workers were needed for this effort. If we were lucky, we'd find someone who needed us to shock.

Usually a group of farmers would work together to haul the oat bundles and process them. These groups of farmers were known as "threshing rings." Most farmers had switched to combines now so there weren't many threshing rings left but we knew there were a few up towards Fulda, north of Worthington.

Not long after sun up in early July, four of us piled into Bruce's car and headed north. We hadn't driven too far when we spied a farmer with a horse-drawn binder cutting oats. The binder machine cuts the oats and gathers the stalks into a bundle and then ties the bundle with twine. We stopped and asked if he needed someone to shock for him. He did but only wanted two. He gave directions to Bruce and Randy to where he knew other farmers in the ring were also cutting oats. Bruce and Randy left and my brother, Kerry and I climbed the fence and the farmer showed us how he wanted the shocks made.

"Pick up two bundles in each hand." The farmer grabbed four bundles by the twine ties as he walked between the rows of bundles. "Once you get to the next two, set the first ones down like this." He bent a knee to support the four bundles, making a sort-of tent.

"Be sure that the opening is on the west side to catch the wind." He grabbed another pair of bundles and added them to the shock, orienting them with the first four. He grabbed a two more bundles and put them on top with the grain heads pointing south and the straw end pointing north. "That's how I need it done. Are you ready?"

We nodded and he walked over to the binder, climbed up and with a click of his tongue to the horses he was off leaving us to the learn how to shock. We were smart enough to bring gloves and hats but hadn't thought about water. We worked hard and luckily, the farmer had a jug of water with him on the binder.

About ten o'clock the farmer's wife pulled into a driveway along-side the field and carried a basket lunch up to the fence. We all sat down to a baloney sandwich, pint fruit jar of Kool Aid and a piece of cake. We rested for a few minutes and then went back to shocking. We never gained on the binder and the bundles stretched endlessly. At noon we rode on the binder up to the farm house for dinner. I don't remember what we ate but we were hot, hungry and tired and the whole afternoon with thousands of bundles loomed so food and shade was welcome bliss.

We worked until suppertime when Bruce and Randy showed up. The farmer asked if we were coming back the next day. We said yes. We did come back and we did finish the field. We were paid a dollar an hour and each pocketed a twenty dollar bill for our effort.

We never shocked oats again and all of the threshing rings disappeared long ago. It's a memory I cherish but an experience I don't want to repeat!

Blizzard Warning

I started my senior year at Worthington High in 1955. I'd gotten a job working part time at the bowling alley and now earned enough money to make owning a car possible, even necessary. A few weeks before Christmas, I became the proud owner of a 1939 Ford four-door sedan. I bought it for $75 from a guy who worked part-time at Obie O'Brien's Standard Station which was next to the bowling alley on Oxford Street. The former owners of the car were an older couple in Adrian who must have taken exceptional care of it because everything worked, even the clock. Well, almost everything worked except the Southwind gasoline heater, a notoriously unreliable optional add-on, which I guessed was why they were selling it! Anyway, they were getting a newer car and their son knew I was looking for a car so he stopped into the bowling alley and we made a deal. I didn't care about the heater; I'd get different one from the Junk yard. The important thing was I finally had a car and was free to go wherever I wanted whenever I wanted. When I got the car home, while rummaging thru the trunk, I discovered there was a set of tire chains. I didn't think much about them but noted they might come in handy someday if the weather turned bad.

When Christmas vacation started I drove over to Lakefield and paid a visit to Schultz's Salvage Yard where I bought a fine heater from Wilhelm Schultz and then stopped at Loren Woodkey's garage and we installed it. I had now conquered winter and was ready with a car that was warm and comfortable.

I drove it around town and showed it off to my friends, most of whom were polite but unimpressed; it was a black four-door family sedan, definitely the low end of cool when it came to teenage cars! John Fitch had a big black 1939 Buick four-door sedan with dual spare tires mounted in the front fenders giving it gangster car cool. Gile Bixby had a 1947 Chrysler New Yorker coupe with a long, sleek hood for elegant cool. Don Barrier often drove one of his Dad's used cars like the bright yellow 48 Ford convertible coupe' and sometimes was allowed to drive around in their red, topless, sports car that rumbled loudly; both very, very cool. Brad Dickey drove a dark blue 1947 Chevy Fleetline with a "shaved" hood, lowered rear end, custom grill, fender skirts was the coolest. My old, un-sleek, four-door, family sedan never generated a single blip on the cool meter; it didn't even have a radio; just a working clock and a good heater.

I was dating Mary, a girl from Fulda, and having total control of my transportation needs gave a real boost to my social opportunities. Within a few days of my purchase, I drove down to the Thompson Hotel to use their lobby pay phone; a long distance call to Fulda only cost a quarter at the pay phone, a cheap way to have a private conversation. Luckily, Mary was also enjoying the leisure of the Christmas holidays from school and she answered the phone. I arranged a date for the next night. I've forgotten what we did that evening but most likely we met up with a group of her Fulda high school classmates at the local café and just hung around talking and enjoying each other. By the time I dropped Mary off and headed home it was starting to snow.

As I headed south on Highway 59 the snowfall increased; the flakes became larger and larger and with no wind they dropped straight down, quickly blanketing the road in a thickening layer of fluffy white and almost totally blocking forward vision. I hadn't driven more than a few miles before it became almost impossible to see where I was driving. In the dark, the smooth white blanket and heavy snowfall blotted out every landmark and hid the edges of the road. I slowed down and then slowed down even more. I rolled down my window and stuck my head out but that didn't work at all. Part of the problem was the glow of the headlights reflecting off the nearly solid wall of white snowflakes.

Unable to figure out where I was going, I decided to try a somewhat novel solution. Automobiles as old as my 1939 Ford were largely still equipped with choke knob and a throttle knob. The throttle knob acted like cruise control on modern cars; pull it out to the desired speed and away you go. Of course the safety feature of touching the brakes to disconnect it wasn't going to come for many years. I pulled the knob out until I was going about 15 miles an hour; then opened the car door and got on the running board (another feature of older cars that has long since disappeared) and steering with my right hand continued my journey, creeping slowly toward Worthington. I was able to see better by looking over the headlights and after a few miles the snow let up enough so I could get back in and drive normally. It was a surreal experience and, as far as I remember, I never met a single car during that heavy snowfall.

* * *

Before our holiday vacation ended Worthington was treated to one of Southwestern Minnesota's famous winter blizzards. When snow mixes with the strong winds from the northwest that sweep unobstructed across the Dakota prairies the result is a furious maelstrom. Snow, whipped into a blinding fury, blots out everything; quickly building huge drifts that swallow parked cars, roads and driveways. Buildings that block the wind are quickly surrounded by drifts that sometimes climb to roof-top heights. Nearly everyone stays indoors where it's safe and warm. I had a car with chains in the trunk and a good heater; so you could reason that I'd be safe and warm in my car and didn't need to stay home!

I called LeRoy and asked if he'd like to go out and enjoy riding around in a blizzard; explaining that I had a good set of tire chains and it would be a more exciting way to break the monotony of watching a blizzard than looking at it through a living room window. LeRoy, every bit as thoughtful and cautious as I was, quickly said yes. I told him I'd be over as soon as I figured out how to get the tires chains mounted. I told Mom and Dad that I was going over to LeRoy's. Putting on warm clothes I headed outside and grabbed a shovel. We didn't have a garage so my car was parked in the street and was already partially buried. I dug quickly and didn't have any trouble getting the chains on. The blizzard hadn't yet reached its full fury so the temperature, while dropping fast, was high enough that my car started easily. The chains worked marvelously and I barged my way through the deepening snow with ease, arriving quickly at LeRoy's house. As I turned into the alley that ran alongside the house I could see LeRoy looking out the side door. He was already wearing a coat and stocking cap and pushed the door open, jumped down the steps and hopped into my car.

"Now what?" LeRoy grinned with an excited twinkle in his eyes.

"Let's drive downtown and see what's moving."

I drove the rest of the way down the alley and turned toward Tenth Street. There were a few deeper drifts in the alley but the chains worked their magic and we bulled right through. I was delighted.

We ploughed our way up Tenth but nothing was stirring. Driving around in a blizzard isn't really a very interesting way to spend your time. There's nobody out and about, everything is closed so you can't stop and talk to anyone. Everything's buried under snow so there isn't anything to look at. Boredom fighting is, in its self, pretty boring; but we drove on aimlessly. Our lonely trek led us around Lake Okabena, past Cherry Point then north along Whiskey Ditch and then up Oxford Street. We were climbing up the hill just west of McMillian Street when the engine raced and the car suddenly slowed then stopped.

LeRoy and I looked at each other our faces frozen in shock. I shifted into low gear and tried to get moving; no luck. I shifted into reverse; same result. LeRoy opened his door and stepped out into the gale. He was back inside in a flash already coated with snow.

"You've lost the right chain."

We both just sat there for a few seconds pondering our fate. There are three possible outcomes from losing a chain in deep snow. If the outside link came unsnapped, the chain will be hanging around the axel behind the wheel and can be reattached with a little work. If the inside link came loose the chain may be laying right next to the wheel where it is easily found and can be reattached. If both links came loose the chain may be anywhere under the snow. We both got out of the car and started looking for the chain. It was obvious that the third possibility was what happened. When I put the chains on I had just thrown the shovel in the trunk so we had something to dig in the snow with. We took turns digging; swapping places in the car to warm up. We knew that if we didn't find the chain we were stuck there until someone came along, maybe a snow plow or truck, and it didn't look like anyone would be coming by for a while.

Our searching finally paid off. LeRoy found the chain about fifty feet behind the car. Now all we had to do was dig out under the car and reattach the chain. Once we could spread the chain out behind the wheel, LeRoy and I both pushed the car backwards over the chain and pulled it up over the tire and reattached it. We were tired, wet and cold. We were also aware that challenging a blizzard needlessly was a pretty stupid stunt even if it did relieve boredom; we went straight home.

* * *

That lesson didn't really last though. About ten years later on a wintry Friday evening, my wife, Lonni, and I bundled up our two small boys and left Minneapolis for a weekend visit to her family's farm just south of Rushmore. The weather forecast was for snow but we thought it wouldn't amount to much. By the time we passed Mankato the wind had picked up and it was snowing pretty hard. Between Windom and Wilder the drifts were creeping over the road and becoming pretty deep. From Heron Lake to Worthington the country's wide open, mostly flat without much for wind breaks so there weren't many snow drifts over the road; we didn't even think about stopping at my folks in Worthington; foolishly we just kept plowing along.

By the time we turned south at Rushmore the blizzard was in full force with visibility near zero and deep drifts all the way across the road. I had to drive faster than I should have to make sure I could "buck" through the drifts. I knew what to expect as we approached Lonni's parents farm which sits atop a hill on the east side of the road surrounded by a dense grove of trees. The driveway was likely drifted in so I drove as fast as I thought I could and still make the turn into the driveway. I made the turn. The driveway was filled in by a drift about four feet deep and way too long to just blow through. The drift was high enough to bury the car up to windowsills making it impossible to open the doors! Lonni's folks saw our headlights and Harm, her father, plowed his way on foot out the driveway to our rescue. We handed the boys out the car windows and then I climbed out. After we got the kids to the house, Harm and I went back to the car, pulled the luggage out of the trunk, got the passenger side door open far enough for Lonni to get out, rolled up the driver's window and waded back to the house leaving the car buried in the drift until morning.

I'd never seen Lonni's dad mad before and I've never seen him madder than he was that night. Germans aren't very vociferous so Harm didn't really say too much but wondered aloud how I could be so stupid to haul two little children out in a storm.

He was right; it was pretty stupid.

Town and Country

Once every six weeks, St. Mary's College, in Winona, sent a dozen or so nursing students to Worthington to learn about "rural nursing." When word spread that a new group of female college students had arrived, you couldn't get a parking spot within two blocks of their dormitory behind the hospital. Every young swain in town hustled over there to view the new bevy of young ladies and make on effort lure one of them out on a date. If we were successful, we then faced the problem of where to go and what to do. The first date was usually something safe, like a movie at the State Theater followed by a Burger Basket at Mike's Spaghetti House. If there was the second date, we now had to overcome Worthington's relative paucity of active entertainment opportunities. There was a bowling alley, a roller rink, a movie theater, a summer drive-in theater and a couple of restaurants but not much of anything else. We struggled to discover venues with more exciting atmospheres. Our most reliable option was a road trip and, for us, that usually meant heading to Round Lake for an evening at the Town and Country Club.

The Town and Country Club was part saloon, part road house, part after-hours joint and part gambling den. The décor was sparse and somewhat run-down but that just added to the appeal. It was also cheap and, if the scene was right, we could also drink something other than root beer. A long, narrow space with a bar on your right and booths on your left as you walked in. Once past the bar, the room opened up revealing a modest dance floor with a juke box on the far wall. A large booth in the far right-hand corner blocked the view of the restrooms. That booth was most often used as a center for poker games later in the evenings. I guess we choose the place because it had an air of wildness about it that we felt would appeal to the refined ladies from St. Mary's! We took dates there from time to time but we went there mostly to hang out with our friends, play cards and enjoy ourselves.

Most nights there was a crowd of men at the end of the bar playing a card game called "Huckly Buck," a gambling version of Buck Euchre. One warm summer evening one of the players at the bar was a man nick-named "Toughy." He was well built and by his looks, deserved the name. As the evening grew late the game continued unabated and soon a woman appeared at the end of the bar. She was wearing a shapeless cotton dress, wasn't wearing makeup and her hair hung loosely which made her seem small and meek. Approaching Toughy, she put her hand on his arm and pleaded softly, "Toughy, can we go home now I'm tired."

Toughy roughly pushed her away and snarled, "I'm playing cards. Get away! Leave me alone." He pushed her hand off his arm.

The woman quietly disappeared back into the booth area and Toughy continued to play. A short while later the woman reappeared only this time she was carrying a half-full bottle of vodka. She walked up to Toughy, grabbed his arm and pulled him around so he was facing her.

"We're going home," she said as she swung the bottle and hit him alongside the head.

Toughy went over backwards and the woman grabbed his shirt and dragged him toward the door. I never saw Toughy again.

I was enrolled at Worthington Community College and worked at the Oxford Bowl nights. In late spring I finished work about 11 PM. Friends Jim and Denny bowled on a team that night and they hung around until I finished work and was free to leave. We decided to head for Round Lake to see if there was anything going on at the Town and Country. When we got there, the place was pretty quiet but Denny managed to grab a seat in the Huckly Buck game at the end of the bar. It was a warm night and with nothing going on inside; Jim and I went outside and sat down on the curb to enjoy a cigarette. The evening solitude was soon interrupted by the sound of car coming into town at high speed, noisily sliding around the corner and speeding up the street toward us. It slammed to a stop right in front of us and without a word, Denny's wife, jumped out, slammed the car door, gave us an angry look and stomped inside. Jim and I glanced at each other, jumped up and followed her into the club. We didn't know what would happen but we wanted to be there when it did.

Denny was sitting at the bar, facing away from the door and hadn't the slightest idea what was coming toward him. The angry wife strode up behind Denny, grabbed his arm and swung him around to face her. She then wound up and gave him a slap that could probably have been heard outside. Denny blinked and without much of a pause, turned back to face the other card players.

"Gentlemen, I'd like you to meet my wife."

Denny then turned, took his wife's hand and, without a word, they walked out the door. Both Jim and I felt relieved that we'd escaped her wrath.

The bar at the Town and Country sold 3.2 beer and set-ups (a soft drink in a glass over ice cubes). As far as I can recall, they never knowingly served beer to minors but the place was usually crowded with underage patrons. It was normal for a number of neighbors to complaint about noise, boisterous behavior and noisy late night traffic. Because the town of Round Lake was too small for a local police department, Sheriff Sandy Deuel was required to respond to quell the nuisances that sprang forth from the Town and Country. In order to mollify the complainers, Sheriff Deuel was required to pay an occasional evening visit to the club.

We were whooping it up one evening when Finn, the proprietress, jumped up on bar and yelled, "THE SHERIFF IS COMING! EVERYONE UNDER TWENTY ONE OUT THE BACK DOOR!"

I think someone tipped off the club before Sheriff Deuel arrived just to make sure there wouldn't be any observable lawbreaking that would increase the Sheriff's workload and unfairly punish Finn.

Without any further urging, we all made a mad dash through the kitchen and out the back door into the alley where we scattered to our cars, hoping for a clean get away.

One of the revelers, Randy, often parked in the alley behind the club. There was a small grocery store next to the Town and Country and a vacant lot just beyond the grocery store. The night of the raid, Randy ran out the back door, jumped in his car, started it, sped up the alley and, as he usually did, hung a quick left around the grocery store for a short-cut across the vacant lot to the street. Much to Randy's surprise, he discovered that a new construction project had started on the vacant lot. He made this discovery as his car plunged into the pit of a freshly dug basement! Randy wasn't hurt. His car wasn't damaged. Everyone heading out the back door heard the thud of Randy's car as it fell into the basement pit. We all gathered around to enjoy Randy's embarrassment and help him pull the car back out of the hole.

Most evenings at the club were more sedate. Usually, about 10PM, Finn would bring out a wool army blanket and spread it over the big booth in the back corner. This meant a few of the regular poker players had showed up and were ready to play. I was more of a kibitzer than a player but sat in a few times. There were regulars, the farmer in bib overalls who kept money in every pocket and would always dig out a few wadded bills from a different pocket every time he bet. A law man from someplace in northern Iowa was also a regular; I think he was a county sheriff. I've forgotten who the rest were but it was usually the same faces.

If there was an open seat, passersby often slid in and joined the game. On night, Billy, a fellow I knew from Worthington, sat down and started to play. Billy was far from an experienced poker player but that night he couldn't lose; his winnings piled up rapidly, he filled every straight, he turned low pairs into a full house, if someone held queens he held kings. As the game wound down and the players began to glumly swallow their losses and leave the table; Billy ordered a big steak and sat gleefully savoring his winnings as he devoured the steak.

As he finally got up to leave he was heard to remark; "Wow! That was easy, have a fun night, drink, play cards, eat a big steak and I'm going home with way more money than I came in with." With a big smile on his face he gave a happy wave to crowd and swaggered out the door.

It few days passed before Billy came back for more. What he didn't know and would soon learn was that over the long haul, skill and good technique give the experienced poker player an edge over the causal player. The regular crowd in the back booth at the Town and Country Club knew how to play the game. They also played together often enough that they knew a lot about each other's habits and betting patterns. This meant that while every night there were different winners, over the long haul everyone stayed pretty even. Billy's luck stayed hidden on the evening of his return and his poker skills weren't evident either. It didn't take too long before Billy's cash was pretty much gone and he realized there wouldn't be a big streak dinner celebration either. He quietly left the table and I never saw him in the back booth again.

Old Belle St. Mary's

When my brother, Kerry, and I were quite small, Mom and Pop Smith's daughters, Betty and Poodler (her real name was Monica but I knew her only as Poodler), babysat us often. One weekend Dad took Mom along on an overnight trip with the orchestra he played with, leaving us in the capable hands of the Smith sisters. Early on Sunday morning they got us up, dressed us in our best clothes and led us down the street to old St. Mary's Church for Sunday Mass. It may have been their previous experiences with us or maybe just simple caution on their part; for whatever reason they took us up into the choir loft. I most likely had been to church there many times before but my first memory of St. Mary's is the view of the nave and sanctuary from that choir loft.

I've since been in great gothic cathedrals like Notre Dame and Westminster Abbey, stood in the ruined splendor of ancient Irish monasteries, spent a quiet moment in simple country chapels and worshipped in modern churches of steel and glass; all have left an impression but none so vivid as that first panorama from high up in that choir loft. As I peeped over the railing and looked down, the nave seemed enormous, rows and rows of pews marched forward to the high altar in the sanctuary, statues and candles and colored windows and music - I was entranced.

Since we lived so close, the church was a part of our neighborhood playground. Nobody ever locked anything then so we could wander in and out of the church as we pleased. Usually we could manage to pull open the door in the bell tower and climb up to the landing that led into main part of the church. One of us would giggle, or a girl would squeak or we'd hear footsteps echoing on the wooden floor and we'd bolt back down the stairs and back outside like a bunch of scurrying mice.

With walls of brick and a roof and floor of wood, that place seemed almost alive. The building talked with creaks and whispers, shivering and snapping in the cold, radiators gurgling and clanking contentedly, bright and cheerful in the morning, warm and golden in the afternoon, cool on hot days or cozy and inviting when it's wet and cold, always quiet and peaceful but never asleep.

Father Hale (more about him later), laughingly described St. Mary's architectural style as "Bastardized

Romanesque". The side windows had double vertical panes of stained glass rounded at the top and crowned with a small round pane, all set in an arched opening. There was a square bell tower with arched and columned openings in the belfry and topped with a low rounded roof and stout gold cross. There were no bells - the tower was never designed to hold any. The roof was peaked and looked like it was shingled with light brown slate. Inside, the walls were plaster and the ceiling was barrel vaulted. The interior was decorated using stencils, a common practice when it was built; borders of interlocking designs ran around the tops of the walls and up and down the flat columns between the windows. A large blue semi-circle, also bordered with stencils, backed the altar. I used to study those intricate designs and try to figure out how they were made, it wasn't until many years later that I discovered the answer - maybe I should have paid more attention to what was going on instead of staring at the walls.

The light colored walls and ceiling changed color during the day, they started out pale blue early in the dawn, changed to peach in mid-morning, became beige at mid-day, rose in the afternoon and ocher in the evening. Each color seemed appropriate for each time of day. Restful blue for early morning Mass, cheerful peach for High Mass on Sunday, untroubled beige for afternoon meditation and somber ocher for the Stations of the Cross and Rosary on Wednesday nights.

The smooth oak pews had little metal hat clips on their backs and unpadded kneelers, providing order and structure - and sore knees. In an arched niche to the front and right of the main altar was a statue of St. Joseph and in a similar niche on the left was a statue of Jesus, the Sacred Heart. In front of St. Joseph was a small statue of St. Teresa, the Little Flower, and a rack for votive candles (real candles, not the little glass votive lights used now). A large crucifix hung on the side wall just in front of the statue of Jesus. The main altar sat on a raised platform. The altar was white with gold trim, simple, almost without decoration. A plain white statue of the Blessed Virgin sat atop the altar in an arched enclosure. A wooden communion rail separated the altar from the nave.

After that first view from the choir loft I spent most of my church going on the main floor. I liked to sit on the end of the pew, on the main aisle where I could see what was going on and where I could run my hand along the rounded cap at the end of the pew. When I lost interest in the ceremony (which must have been quite a lot since I remember much about what things looked like and only a few snippets of the hundreds of sermons I sat through), I would play with one of the metal hat clips. I imagine there were dozens of small boys, hunched down in their pews during the sermon, furiously working their private hat clip fantasies.

The Latin Mass was still in use then; the devout followed along in their missal or fingered a rosary. The congregation remained silent for most of the Mass save for an occasional "amen". During the summer we'd recite the Litany of the Saints, as a prayer for good crops. I can still hear the Gregorian rhythm of those names - Santa Lucia, *ora pro nobis*, Santa Cecilia, *ora pro nobis* ... Latin added mystery and solemnity to the ceremony.

The wooden communion rail had a cloth backing that was pulled over the top of the railing, like a table cloth, when communion was distributed. Since you had to fast, no food or water after midnight, there weren't usually a large number of communicants except during lent. There was no singing during Mass, except at High Mass and then only by the choir. On Wednesday night devotions we sang hymns - mostly dull Latin ones like "Tantum Ergo".

Father Hale was a good preacher and his sermons were interesting enough to keep your attention and, on hot summer Sundays, they were brief and to the point. Christmas always seemed to inspire his best efforts. I know memory plays tricks but it seemed like every Midnight Mass on Christmas Eve brought forth an inspiring sermon, a beautiful ceremony and when we emerged into the night, giant snowflakes floated serenely downward and you knew that there truly could be Peace on Earth.

After Mass on Sunday the McCoy brothers sold Minneapolis Star-Journal newspapers at the bottom of the front steps, once home delivery started they were out of business.

There was a large lawn on the east side of the church, with a row of elm trees next to the Rectory. A sidewalk ran along the side of the church and over to the Rectory. We'd often use the lawn for neighborhood games and frequently saw the priests clad in black cassock and biretta, pacing back and forth along the sidewalk reciting their daily "office." What a tranquil scene that was - long late afternoon shadows, the "chirp" of nighthawks wheeling overhead, the calm perfumed summer air and the rhythmic swaying cassock of the head-bowed meditant.

My first memory picture of Father Hale is one of him spading the convent garden, clad in an old white shirt and baggy brown pants; his hair was coal black then, just like his eyebrows. Doug Fiola and I had wandered over to climb in the apple tree behind the church. Father saw us and called us over. He leaned on the spade, mopped his forehead with a large white handkerchief, lit a Camel cigarette and we talked for a while - I've long forgotten the subject. His Irish charm was as good with little boys as it was with everyone else, I always thought of him as a friend after that day.

I saw him angry only twice, both times it was during Sunday Mass. Once, a few older boys in the choir loft began fooling around and Father stopped the service and ordered them to leave the church so we could enjoy our meditation rather than their horseplay. The other time was over "early leavers". After communion there is a brief period of silent meditation, a final prayer and then we are dismissed. A few church goers would slip out during the meditation right after communion or sometimes even during the distribution of communion. Maybe they wanted to be sure to get a paper before the McCoy's ran out or maybe they wanted to avoid the crowd at the door - who knows why they would leave five minutes early. On the fateful day, Father whirled around, faced the culprits and THUNDERED angrily at their slothfulness, cowardice and bad manners. Most, shamefacedly sat back down. It was a good many Sundays before anyone got brave enough to leave early.

Both Kerry and I became acolytes (mass servers) when we were eight or nine. Sister Mary Julia, Father Hale's sister, taught us the Latin prayers. When he was old enough, my younger brother, Tim, also joined the ranks. After a few years we gained enough experience to become part of a cadre of servers that stayed together for several years - Larry and Jerry McCoy, Jerry and Joe Roberts, Doug Fiola, Joe and Tom Judge, Tom Mennenga and others whose names I've forgotten. During those years we assisted at most of the major feasts - Midnight Mass at Christmas, Holy Thursday, Good Friday, and Easter Vigil - and did our share of weddings and funerals as well.

On occasion, if we were called upon for extra duty, like two masses back-to back on Sunday, we were rewarded with breakfast at the rectory. Father Hale's housekeeper, Marie Sassen, made the world's best cinnamon rolls and sugar cookies. Once, Father had me sit at the head of the table and said I was a Monsignor and to be addressed as "Your Reverence." I think Father Gerber was an assistant then and he joined Father Hale in the mock papal elevation of a red-headed, freckle faced boy to ecclesiastical prominence. I was embarrassed; but not too embarrassed to enjoy Marie's fine breakfast!

We were scheduled to serve morning Masses for a week at a time, I don't know how we survived. We'd drag ourselves sleepily through the dewy shadows of early morning and trudge slowly up the steep back stairs to the sacristy. From a wardrobe full of cassocks we'd select a likely looking one and put it on - usually too short so we'd have to try again before we got a good fit. Over the black cassock we'd don a white surplice and we were ready - but not yet fully awake.

The priest would arrive and we'd watch as he donned his vestments. First the amice, a kind of bib worn over the back and shoulders and tied on with long cloth strips pulled across the chest and around the waist. Then he put on the Alb, a long sleeved white tunic - something like the caftans that Arabs wear. The rope-like cincture was used like a belt to hold the Alb in place. Depending on the Mass of the day the remaining vestments were colored - red for a martyr's feast day, white for other Saints, violet for Vigils like Advent and Lent, green for the season after Pentecost and black for Masses of for the Dead. The stole, a long scarf, was placed over the neck and crossed the chest, its ends held in place by loops in the cincture. The maniple, a long fringed band of cloth was fastened to the right sleeve just above the wrist with a pin - like a waiters napkin (it represents a napkin which signifies authority). Finally the chasuble, a lose covering that is draped over the body and falls down in folds over the arms. Of all those vestments only the Alb, stole and chasuble seem to have survived Vatican II.

When Father put on the chasuble we had better have the candles lit and the water and wine cruets in place because Mass was about to start. We'd bravely stand in the doorway to the sanctuary ready to give a yank on the bell rope at Father's signal. He'd nod, we'd pull and Mass was underway.

I enjoyed the chance to serve and continued until I left home. My last function was at the dedication of the new St. Mary's church in 1959. I was the cross bearer and led the first procession up the main aisle and into the sanctuary. A few weeks after that I paid a call on Father Hale to bid him farewell; I was moving to Minneapolis and leaving Worthington for good.

In 1957 St. Mary's congregation elected to build a new, larger church. The old church wasn't very accessible and was showing its age. It came down in 1958. Photo courtesy Nobles County Historical Society.

STORIES TOO GOOD TO BE TRUE

Memories of the past are wonderful adventures but sometimes we remember things that probably either didn't happen or did happen but not nearly in the same way we remember them. I long thought there was a fireworks explosion during one of the 4th of July celebrations on Lake Okabena. Research has proved that I was mistaken. That memory failure led me to decide I'd create that event and a few others just for the sheer joy of bringing the Worthington of my youth back to life.

These stories are fiction and none of the main characters are real. From time to time I have included a few real names whenever I felt their presence added context to the story I have done so. I also tried to recreate the atmosphere of Worthington during the middle 1950s. I hope these stories are enjoyable to read as much as they were enjoyable to create. I will warn you that there is a chance that some truth may, from time-to-time, have slipped in.

If Turkeys could Fly

My junior year at Worthington High School was underway in the fall of 1954. Fall had barely arrived, bright and warm; so early in the morning on Wednesday, September 22nd, my attention switched from school to Turkey Day.

Worthington's annual King Turkey Day celebration is a cherished tradition designed to boost the city and give us a chance to enjoy ourselves with a parade, street carnival, political speeches, fireworks and dancing. It draws amazing crowds and is eagerly anticipated.

There is no school on Turkey Day so I got up a little late. A big tent in front of the Armory would be serving free pancakes to a large crowd and parking could be tough so I washed and dressed quickly, told mom and dad I'd be gone all day and didn't know exactly when I'd be home, ran out to my car and headed downtown; I figured if I got there early enough I could find a place to park by the depot. Sure enough I found a spot by the co-op elevator.

Downtown bustled as I wound my way on foot down Tenth Street and turned left at Third Avenue. The street was crowded; food stands and carnival game booths were opening up and the atmosphere was already noisily festive. I could see the pancake tent in front of the Armory with a line already stretching down Ninth Street; the free pancake tradition always draws an early crowd. Hoping some of my friends would be there; I just got in line and peered inside looking for familiar faces. I didn't have to wait long as Dan punched my arm as he walked by.

"LaVoy and Jon aren't too far behind. I saw them as I was parking my car."

"What are you driving?" I asked.

"Dad let me take a '48 Ford Convertible he just bought at the Valley Springs auction. It's bright yellow; it's a killer!"

Dan's dad is a user car dealer so every once in a while Dan would show up with exotic wheels. On a day like today a convertible would draw "women" like a magnet. LaVoy and Jon spotted us as they came around the corner toward the tent. Dan and I were swept inside by the fast-moving line. Hap Ehlers handed each of us a paper plate with two pancakes. We pushed our way to a couple of empty spaces at a table. Jon and LaVoy squeezed in alongside and Dan told them about the convertible. Jon grinned mischievously and LaVoy rolled his eyes. We all knew that Turkey Day drew a crowd from far and wide including "women" we'd never met, so hunting with a convertible for "bait" could be wild fun. We were ready! Two pancakes don't last long and we were quickly out of the tent and into the crowd. We stopped for a minute and watched a guy selling "miracle car wax."

LaVoy shook his head. "It's just paraffin and mineral oil. The first rain will wash it off."

The salesman kept up his patter. "Not even fire will take it off. Watch this." He shot a stream of lighter fluid onto the car hood he was polishing, flipped out a cigarette lighter and with a whoosh, the hood exploded in flames which quickly burned out. The salesman gleamed in triumph. We walked on leaving the awed cluster of rubes behind.

We were headed down Ninth Street past the court house. We had some time to kill before we could go back for more pancakes, they had to change servers; Hap Ehlers would recognize us and kick us out of the tent.

"Let's see what's going on at Emil's." Jon was a good pool player and always wanted to go to Emil's Pool Hall. Tucked in below Ray's Café, Emil's was the antithesis of Meier Brother's Tavern and Pool Hall on Tenth Street. Open the door to Emil's and you were immersed in loud talk, boastful physical action and "dirty" pool. Meier's, on the other hand, was quiet, sedate, and respectful and boasted both a billiard and snooker table.

We bolted down the stairs and stepped into Emil's smoky gloom. Someone in the back corner by an open table shouted to Jon and waved a cue. Jon waved back and walked over to the cue rack and picked out one he recognized. Emil chalked in the time as Jon walked back to the corner. LaVoy lit a cigarette and hopped up on an empty stool to watch. Dan and I each asked Emil for a bottle of Pepsi Cola and a Pearson's Salted Nut Roll candy bar, calling for the combination by their "in" name "a Pepsi and a Pearce."

Jon won the lag and made the first three pockets before missing his fourth shot. The stranger couldn't compete and Jon won four straight games. We finished our pop and LaVoy put out his cigarette. As the stranger paid for the table we headed back upstairs into the bright sunlight. Hoping that they'd changed servers at the Pancake Tent, we headed back there for another stack.

By the time we'd finished our second stack of pancakes, the power plant whistle announced noon and downtown was crowded with revelers; Tenth Street was already closed off from Ninth Avenue all the way to Second Avenue.

"With this big a crowd, maybe we can get someone to buy us a beer at Meier's," Dan said. We decided we'd had enough pancakes and headed up Tenth.

"Yeah, I think I can get one of the guys in the back to help us out." Jon played at lot of pool in Meier's back room; his Dad's hardware store was just across the alley.

We pushed our way down Tenth Street into the crowded tavern and threaded our way to the pool room in back. The pool room wasn't as crowded as the bar but still bustled with activity; we had to scramble to find four chairs. Jon spotted a friend.

"I need a buck each." Jon held out his hand. We each gave him a dollar and watched hopefully as he wound his way around the tables. The deal was struck for four bottles of beer and the guy disappeared into the bar. We waited nervously until he reappeared carrying a tray topped with four frosty bottles. Keeping a watchful eye and trying to look invisible, we enjoyed the forbidden luxury of a cold bottle of suds. Luckily, we were just taking our last swigs when Jon spotted a friend of his Dad step in from the alley through the back door. We quickly set the beer bottles on the floor and headed out the front onto the crowed street.

"Now what?" LaVoy asked.

"It's almost time for the parade. Let's see if we can get a good spot to watch." I was curious to see if the Fulda High School Band had replaced their drum Majorette, Verdelle. She led the band costumed as an Indian princess complete with a feathered war bonnet, fringed buckskinned skirt, vest and beaded buckskin boots. She was also an excellent baton twirler. Verdelle graduated the year before; her hoped for replacement had a big war bonnet to fill!

We crowded in at the front of Rickbeil's Hardware. LaVoy said he was hungry and pointed in the direction the Popcorn Wagon.

"I'll bet they're serving hot dogs. Give me some cash and I'll us some."

We each gave LaVoy a dollar and he disappeared into the mob. It was only a couple of minutes and he was back with an armload of hot dogs and bags of popcorn.

"The dogs were only a quarter so I got us each three and a bag of popcorn too."

The beer followed by hot dogs and popcorn on the curb was pure bliss. We were now ready to enjoy the parade. As we wolfed down the last bite of hot dog, we could see the turkey flock gobbling its way up the street, herded by straw-hatted wranglers wearing bib overalls, polka-dotted bandanas and wielding sticks tipped with red flags. The pre-parade publicity claimed there would be over a thousand turkeys in the flock but it didn't seem like that many to us. We would have ignored the statue of King Turkey that followed the turkeys but cheered wildly as "Miss Worthington," Shirley Fischer waved from high atop the giant bird. Shirley had graduated in the spring and was probably headed away to college. Our collective opinion was that as good looking and talented as she was, winning the title "Miss Minnesota" was a real long shot; we wished her well anyway.

Now we settled in to wait for the Fulda marching band. We cheered wildly when the wagon carrying the Eddie Skeets Orchestra rolled by as they played the Meadow Lark Polka. Dad saw me, and waved his trumpet at me. I waved back. More floats and more bands but then we spotted the war bonnet headdress swaying up the street.

The new Fulda marching princess did not disappoint. She marched with short jumping steps that mimicked those of Indian dancers. As she marched she swayed and waved her feathered war bonnet headdress side to side. None of us recognized her but we agreed she made a very, very good marching princess. With her passage we lost interest in the parade and slid around the corner to Second Avenue and then up the alley back to Third and the carnival. We wandered around the carnie games but nothing seemed worthwhile enough to spend money on. Why spend two dollars to win a kewpie doll worth about ten cents.

I asked if anyone wanted to listen to Governor Orville Freeman's speech on the courthouse steps. All I got was glares from Dan and Jon but LaVoy seemed interested. We decided to skip the Governor and look for other opportunities.

"There's the Turkey Day Button drawing at the court house after the speeches. They're giving away twenty-five turkeys too. I bought a button so let's head over there to see if I won anything." I was trying hard to escape the cheap carnival game kiosks.

We decided instead to head for the power plant where the parade ended up. We might get lucky and meet some friendly girls. If that didn't work we'd head back to the courthouse.

Jon   spotted it first and gave a low whistle of interest. "Look at all those turkeys." Jon had spotted a large truck parked alongside the power plant and loaded with crates of the turkeys from the parade. The truck was just sitting there, unattended. As we walked by the truck we came upon two crates sitting on the curb behind the truck.

Dan stopped and walked over to the crates. He stood there for a few seconds and then turned. "I have an idea. You guys stay here and I'll go get my car; I'm just down the hill and won't be a minute."

None of the rest of us said anything but I think we all realized that there was the possibility that mischief was brewing.

Dan pulled up in the convertible. "I'll put the top down while you guys put those two cages in the trunk." Dan got out, unlocked the trunk and then started folding down the top; a perfect cover-up for the turkey loading. We quickly shoved the crates in and slammed the trunk shut. Dan finished taking the top down and we all got in.

"Now what?" LaVoy asked. "We drive around and offer girls a free turkey if they get in the car?"

"I've got a better idea if we can make it work." Dan gave us a cryptic smile. "First let's see if we can drive up to the courthouse. I think there's a back entrance behind the jail where we can drive right up to the door; if it isn't locked we can get inside."

"Why the courthouse?" Jon asked. "What can we do there? The place will be crawling with people."

"Don't get too far ahead. First we have to find out if we can get in." Dan was already turning in behind the jail and up to the back door at the courthouse. Everyone was listening to Governor Freeman's speech and the area around the back door was deserted. LaVoy jumped out and tried the door. It was open! Dan scrambled around to the back and opened the trunk.

"LaVoy, look inside and see if the coast is clear," Dan hollered as he pulled a turkey crate out of the trunk.

LaVoy disappeared inside then quickly reappeared and waved us in. I grabbed a crate and headed for the door with Dan close behind. There were four turkeys in each crate which made the crates heavy and awkward. It was obvious that if we carried them any distance it would take two of us for each crate.

"What about the car? Can we leave it here?" Jon asked Dan.

Dan just shrugged. We were inside in a small entry way and now needed to know what Dan was planning before we headed out into the main hall with two crates full of turkeys.

"We've got to find a way to the roof. I want to see if these turkeys can fly."

LaVoy exhaled loudly and pulled open the inner door and disappeared. We waited, peering into the courthouse lobby.

LaVoy quickly reappeared, pulled the door wide and held it open. "The place is empty. We should be able to get to the second floor easy enough but I didn't see any way up to the roof."

"Let's go for it," said Dan as he picked up a corner of the first crate.

Jon grabbed the other end and I picked up the second one. We pushed through the door and hustled to the stairs leading up the second floor. Mostly court rooms, the second floor was completely deserted. Dan walked ahead trying doors as he went.

"I found it," he said in a stage whisper as he ran back to pick up the crate.

The stairs were narrow, dark and steep. The only light was from a small window in the door at the top. As Dan reached the top of the stairs he pushed on the door to the roof.

"Shit! It's locked." We sagged with disappointment. "Wait, there's a hook." Dan flipped the hook and we burst onto the roof.

"Get down, the people across the street can see us." Jon let go of the crate and crouched. We all followed his lead and crouched down. Lowering ourselves we pulled the crates as close to the edge of the roof as we could without being seen. LaVoy lay down on his stomach and slid forward just far enough so he could see over the edge. He lay still for a minute and then slid back and rolled over.

"The speakers are done and they're getting ready to start giving away the turkeys." LaVoy rolled away from the edge and sat up. "How do we get away once we dump the birds?"

"I'll go open the door down the stairs. We'll leave the crates and run down as fast as we can once we do the turkey day dump!" Jon smiled as he crawled over to the door and pulled it open.

Jon and Dan were examining the crates, figuring out how to open them and how to get the turkeys out. We wouldn't have time to pull them out one at a time; we'd have to get them all out at once. Dan slowly pushed a crate up to the edge of the roof and motioned to LaVoy to do the same with the other. Dan gave a wicked smile as he grasped the latch at the end of the crate and the end dropped open. LaVoy followed his lead and opened the other crate. The turkeys crouched quietly not knowing that they were about to experience the miracle of flight. Dan and I grabbed the back of one crate, LaVoy and Jon grabbed the other.

"On three, lift up the crate and shake. Don't get close enough to the roof so anyone can see who you are. One. Two. Three." All four of us lifted and shook the crates. The bewildered turkeys fell out and tumbled downward. The birds managed to flap and flutter and a couple righted themselves enough to glide but mostly they fell like feathered bombs, slowing their fall just enough to avoid killing the startled spectators gazing upwards in paralyzed amazement. The crowd of several hundred people packing the lawn in front of the courthouse and spilling out onto Tenth Street was a sight we didn't expect. We looked downward over the edge; momentarily mesmerized by the spreading chaos below.

"Run!" Dan shouted.

The spell broken, we bolted for the door, raced down the stairs, flew down the next flight and through the hallway to the outside door. We were lucky that the crowd in front of the courthouse was so stunned that they didn't start searching for the culprits in time to foil our getaway. We piled into the convertible. Dan started the engine and drove sedately down the hill, behind the jail and pulled slowly onto Ninth Street.

"We're pretty obvious in a yellow convertible. No sense drawing more attention by driving too fast." Dan smiled. "Let's go to Slater Park and let things cool off." We all grinned foolishly at our daring stunt and our equally daring escape.

In front of the courthouse there was both panic and amusement. The turkeys raced madly about, unable to find an escape route. Brave and foolhardy onlookers chased and grabbed at the passing birds. The lucky ones missed when they grabbed; those who succeeded got pecked by sharp beaks, raked by clawed feet and beaten by flapping wings resulting in a quick release into the arms of another foolish onlooker. The Turkey Day Button Committee stood helplessly on the stage platform not having the faintest idea how to regain control of the event.

Sheriff Sandy Deuel was standing just below the platform when the squawking and flapping of the turkeys raining down on the crowd made him look up. With a mixture of alarm and laughter he caught sight of four heads peering over the edge of the roof at the flock of terrified turkeys performing contorted aerial gymnastics, flapping furiously as they plummeted downward toward him. Before the first bird landed he had already started toward the courthouse doors. His quick action to catch the turkey bombers was thwarted by the Turkey Day Button Committee, scrambling to abandon the platform like sailors abandoning a sinking ship; they rushed down the platform steps enmasse. By the time the sheriff fought his way through them and reached the front doors and burst inside it was too late; we were driving sedately down Ninth Street.

People were already gathering around the lake getting ready for the fireworks. There wasn't a parking space at Slater Park so we just kept going. Jon suggested that we drive to Oxford Street and then down Humiston Avenue heading toward downtown, opposite from the direction we'd fled earlier. It seemed like a good suggestion so that's what we did. Dan stopped the car a block from Tenth Street and we helped him put up the convertible top.

"Now what?" Jon leaned on the front fender.

Dan tugged at Jon's shirt. "Get off the car. If I bring it back scratched Dad will have kittens."

"Let's see if there's anyone a Pratt's," I suggested.

Pratt's Confectionary was a popular school hangout and it was just up the street. We weren't exactly part of the white bucks crowd usually found at Pratts; LaVoy often wore heavy black engineer boots which he had on today, Jon was wearing loafers, Dan had on his signature blue suede shoes and I wore loafers like Jon. We were properly dressed; button down shirts and pants with those cute little beltlets between the back pockets; you can't get anywhere near girls dressed as hoods or bums. We weren't quite as clean-cut but we could have suggested the Four Lads as we strolled toward Pratt's. Dan was the best looking with a stunning "ducktail" hairdo that accented his resemblance to the King, Elvis. Jon was slender and dangerous looking with piercing brown eyes. LaVoy evoked the wildness of Marlon Brando and I brought wavy dark red hair and blue eyes. We were surely "Lady Killers."

As we approached Bill's we could hear the noise of the large crowd in front of the courthouse.

"We better check out the results," suggested LaVoy. We picked up our pace, swept past Bill's without even a side-long glance.

Pandemonium reigned as the milling crowd surged toward and away from the bedraggled birds. Turkey Day Button Committee Chairman Gary Martin finally climbed back up on the platform, walked up to the microphone and whistled loudly. The crowd stopped and looked up at the platform. The bedraggled turkeys slumped where they were, exhausted. A couple of the other members of the Turkey Day Button Committee wandered back onto the platform.

"Who wants a free turkey?" Gary began in an effort to recapture the crowd's attention.

Someone in the crowd shouted, "Do we have to catch'm ourselves?"

Gary started to giggle uncontrollably. With that the crowd began to laugh and yell. Someone grabbed a live turkey and heaved it up on the platform where it just stood there and looked back at the crowd.

The Turkey Day Button Committee did their best. They drew numbers and gave away certificates for a free turkey to the lucky winners. But they never were able to regain control over the boisterous mob. The atmosphere became more and more festive as each number was drawn. As the speeches and ceremonies had dragged on for couple of hours; it now became obvious that a significant number of interested onlookers had strolled over to Ray's Café from time to time for thirst quenching and mood altering beverages.

We had worked our way into the crowd but stayed away from the platform, avoiding the Sheriff just in case he got a good look at us on the roof. We spotted a turkey close by but just looked at each other and walked away. The adrenalin of the afternoon was wearing off and we were gripped by the lethargy of success. Dan said he better get the car back as his dad would be getting anxious about the convertible. Jon, who had diabetes, said he needed to get home to check his blood sugar. I offered to give him a ride and asked LaVoy if he'd like one too. LaVoy nodded. LaVoy worked at Johnson's Bakery and started at 4:30 AM so he wasn't much for staying out late.

When the last number was called out, Sheriff Deuel and a deputy walked onto the platform. Each carried an empty crate that they'd retrieved from the roof. With solemnity, they placed the crates at the front of the platform.

"Why don't a few of you boys each grab one of those birds and bring'm here." The crowd began to drift away.

Savoring our triumph, LaVoy, Jon and I walked toward the depot in silence; retreating so deeply into our individual thoughts that the noise and hubbub of the throng and the clamor of the carnival faded as though someone had turned off the volume and we were strolling through a silent movie scene. Somehow we'd written off our quest to meet and entertain those beautiful and mysterious young "out-of-town women."

I didn't go home though. After dropping off my friends I drove back to the lake and found a place to park by the Campbell Soup plant. The fireworks wouldn't start until after sunset which wasn't too long so I decided to wait by the lake.

The fire department always set up their fireworks launch site at the water intake by the power plant so I found a place to sit close enough to them so I could watch their frantic dance as they set off the aerial rockets. There was no wind and the lake undulated smoothly as the sun sank and twilight swept in. I was half dosing when four girls walked by talking and laughing. Without thinking, I stood up and faced them. One of the quartet looked familiar and I decided I knew who she was.

"Hi," I said. "I think you're Fulda's Marching Indian Princess. Am I right?"

She looked at me cautiously and then smiled; pleased no doubt that someone had recognized her.

"Yes." She paused but the other three girls kept walking. "That's me."

"Are you going to the dance at the Armory?" I asked knowing that one guy alone against four girls doesn't have any chance of connecting; it's always worth a try.

"Maybe."

"Well, I'll look for you and maybe we can have a dance."

"Maybe. I gotta go." She trotted off after her friends.

I stood watching them walk away. The Dancing Indian Princess turned, smiled and gave me a little wave. I waved back. Maybe turkeys can fly after all.

* * *

I've never been able to find any evidence of our efforts that day. I've gone to the Nobles County Library and searched their microfilm files of the Worthington Daily Globe; there's lots of coverage of the 1955 King Turkey Day celebration but no mention of falling birds. A visit to the Nobles County Historical Society also drew a blank. I've asked people who claim to have been there but no one remembers the scene. Dan's dad moved his used car business to Provo, Utah, shortly after Turkey Day and we lost track of Dan and have never been able to find any sign of him since. LaVoy became a civil engineer and moved to the State of Washington. His health has declined over the years and he's not too clear about events as far back as 1954. Jon bravely fought the ravages of Diabetes, going blind, losing both feet and one leg and having a kidney transplant. He finally went on ahead of us in the early nineties.

The 1947 King Turkey Day parade traveling along 10th Street. Photo courtesy Nobles County Historical society.

Nobles County Courthouse shortly after construction, complete with tower and cupola. Photo courtesy Nobles County Historical Society.

Courthouse shortly before its demolition. The cupola is gone and the hipped roof and the front stairs have been removed. The new offices are just barely visible to the left of the old courthouse.

By the Rockets' Red Glare

A light snowfall dusted downtown Worthington and the January wind-chill sent shoppers scurrying for their cars along Tenth Street. As noon approached, a steady procession of local businessmen swept into the Thompson Hotel, stamping their feet, shaking the snow from their coats, taking off their hats and heading upstairs to the large hotel dining room where the Worthington Chamber of Commerce was gathering for their initial Independence Day planning session. They got right to work and had a preliminary list of planned events already put together before the waitresses finished delivering their lunches. Enthusiasm was high and the energy was apparent. The consensus on events reached, discussion turned to establishment of event committees: Chautauqua Band Shell ceremonies, downtown decorations, Lake Okabena boat parade and fireworks. After a short discussion a chairman was selected for each event. The fireworks show would be the most expensive part of the celebration and would require a strenuous fund raising effort. Someone suggested moving the launch site from the lakeshore by the power plant to a barge anchored out in the lake. Everyone liked the idea. The only problem was what could they use as a barge? Now the fireworks committee had two problems to solve; funding the display and acquiring a barge.

Ron Caswell volunteered to take charge of the fireworks committee for the third year in a row. Ron ran an insurance company which gave him some flexibility and he was also a volunteer firemen. The volunteer firemen were responsible for manning the barge and actually setting off the fireworks display.

Shortly after 1:30 the meeting adjourned and the room started to clear. Ron, along with Al Hoodecheck and Gay Hower lingered to discuss fund raising for the fireworks.

"What are we looking at for cost?" Hoodecheck asked Ron. "Now that we've got to fund a barge too."

"Last year we raised forty five hundred. I think I know how we can build a barge without spending too much money' if the city will cooperate. I have a list of last year's donors. Al, if you're ready to start a fund raising effort I'll get you the list."

"I'm ready," Al replied.

It seemed only natural that Worthington would launch its Independence Day celebratory fireworks display over Lake Okabena. Using the lake area just off shore from the power plant as the launch site meant crowds could gather along the shore where the Rock Island Rail Road tracks ran, an ideal grassy expanse to enjoy the spectacle. People who went to the evening band concert could watch the display from the lakeshore along Chautauqua Park.

Gay Hower said he'd talk to Gordy Thompson. Thompson is City Clerk and runs the City Utilities Department. If Gordy was willing to help, building the barge would be much easier.

"I have an idea that might work if Gordy says it's ok." Ron had thought about using the floating sections of dredge pipe for a base of a barge.

Worthington had been dredging Lake Okabena for years, sucking up a thick layer of silt deposited by dust from the "dirty thirties" and spring runoff from Whisky Ditch. Demand for land in the 1890's drove a frenzy of drainage projects to reclaim land too wet to farm. One of those projects widened and deepened Okabena Creek and extended it to a large marsh northwest of Worthington and added a new channel straight into Lake Okabena. The creek and channel, now usually referred to as "Whiskey Ditch," brought more needed water into the lake but also greatly increased the volume of sediment as well. The city dredge, named the "Shawano," was put back into action in 1948 and has been hard at work ever since. Silt sucked up from the lake bottom is pumped through a long string of pipes that float on rafts of fifty-five gallon barrels that lead to a settling area where the silt slurry is discharged as fill.

Ron Caswell already envisioned creating a barge using several of those dredge pipe floats topped with a platform of planks, creating a large and stable barge; perfect for launching the Fourth of July fireworks display.

"Gay, all I need is twelve of those pipe floats and some planks. Gordy should be able to do that for us. I'll get the volunteer firemen to do the carpentry. Piece of cake!"

"I'll get ahold of Gordy right away." Hower clapped Ron on the shoulder and strode to the door. He gave a quick wave and disappeared.

The next day Gay gave Gordy a call, explained what the fireworks committee needed to build a barge. Gordy liked the idea and a deal was quickly agreed to.

January cold gradually gave way to March blizzards and then warm sun began to presage spring. The Kiwanis Club hauled an old car they christened "Lena" out on the lake and began selling "WHEN WILL LENA SINK?" raffle tickets. The July 4th celebration planning complete, attention was already turning to King Turkey Day slated for the third Thursday in September.

Lena sank on April 8th and by April 10th the remaining ice was gone from the lake. The mighty dredge,

Shawano, was freed from its winter mooring at the power plant water intake station and was towed to the center of the lake. Sections of dredge pipe were assembled at the city pasture on the north shore of the lake, wrestled into the water where they were joined into long stings and towed to the waiting dredge. Soon the pipe umbilical was complete and the Shawano rumbled to life, swinging slowly back and forth, devouring the black, mucky silt and pumping it shoreward.

True to his word, Gordy Thompson arranged for the Utilities Department to take pipes off twelve floats, put the floats in the lake and tow them over to the Power Plant. His crew also deposited a pile of planks on the shore for Ron and his crew.

On the last week in June Ron and several of the volunteer firemen went to work. Using chains, they arranged the floats into a three by four rectangle and started nailing the planks in place to form the deck.

Fred Riche and Duane Odenbrett slid a plank in place and Duane knelt down, took a nail from his pouch and gave it a solid blow with his hammer. As he swung the hammer up for the final blow, Fred, carrying the next plank, tripped over Duane and sent his hammer flying overboard into the lake. Duane stood up and gave Fred a playful shove.

"Watch where you're going."

"Sorry, I'll get you another hammer." Fred dropped the plank, jumped ashore, grabbed a hammer and tossed it back to Duane.

The two men finished nailing the plank and started on the next one. By early afternoon the barge was done and the workers stood back and admired the fine job they'd done but didn't see the lonely exposed nail head. Duane, distracted by the loss of his hammer, had moved on, forgetting to drive that one nail flush.

Al Hoodecheck did a superb job of fundraising and the fireworks fund exceeded five thousand dollars. Ron Caswell called Midwest Aerial Displays in May and ordered a total of two hundred bursting pyrotechnic aerial "shells" for what the Worthington Chamber of Commerce announced as the "The Most Spectacular Display of Pyrotechnics."

July 4th dawned balmy and clear with only a gentle breeze from the southwest. By noon, crowds of picnickers filled Chautauqua, Slater and Sunset Parks. At Chautauqua Park, Howard Sevdy brought out his big Chris Craft speed boat and was doing a brisk business giving rides for two dollars apiece. Swimmers filled the beach behind the band shell and children crowded the playground. By late afternoon a few early birds began to setup along the east shore of the lake, spreading blankets, arranging folding chairs and opening picnic baskets. At five o'clock members of the City Band began to stroll on stage at the band shell. At the Boat House on the south shore, several boat parade participants were busily doing final decorative adjustments on their boats before they headed for Cherry Point to form up for the parade. Over fifty boats were expected to participate.

The fireworks barge was already anchored well offshore. Ron Caswell and his crew were unpacking boxes filled with a variety of "shells" and transferring them to the "Okabena," the city dredge workboat, for the short trip to the barge. It took several trips but they were finished by six o'clock. Ron, Fred Ritchie and Duane Odenbrett stayed on the barge where they fastened tubes used to launch the fireworks. There were six tubes on each side of the barge. During the actual display, they would load one set of tubes with shells while the shells on the other side were being launched. Then they would switch sides and repeat. By seven o'clock they had arranged the paper wrapped shells in neat ranks in the order they'd chosen for maximum visual effect. Alongside the stack of fireworks were two fire extinguishers and several life jackets, just in case. Now the crew sat down, dangled their feet over the side of the barge and took a well-earned rest.

Promptly at seven o'clock, Howard Sevdy started the engine on his Chris Craft now sporting a tall mast with a large American flag. Howard slowly idled away from the

Cherry Point dock. The rumble of the Chris Craft exhaust was soon joined by the sounds of fifty boat engines coming to life. The boats quickly fell into line behind Howard. One large runabout was made up to look like a Mississippi steamboat, another was piloted by a man dressed as Abe Lincoln and another sported a covered wagon top. Many were draped in bunting and flew American flags. There was even a runabout converted into a giant papier-mâché turkey! As the colorful procession headed down the north shore of the lake toward Chautauqua Park, the City Band launched into the "Star Spangled Banner" bringing the crowd to their feet and signaling the start of the boat parade.

Music drifting over the lake shore caused the crowd to stir in anticipation. The boat parade slowly came into view as it swung past the park and headed toward the power plant. People along the shore whistled and cheered as the colorful craft crept past. By now the sun was sliding below the horizon and the big orange moon was peeping over the power plant. The City Band ended their concert with the "Washington Post march," finishing with a flourish. As the music died away and twilight settled in, the listless breeze stopped and the lake flattened into a silver mirror ruffled only an occasional motorboat wake. The boat parade ended and boats without lights headed off the lake. Those that remained shut off their engines, turned on their white mooring lights and drifted listlessly on the glassy water.

By nine o'clock everyone was eagerly trying to hurry the slowly deepening twilight and anxiously watching the crew on the barge. At long last, Ron stood up and the watching crowd stirred. Duane Odenbrett took a shell marked "aerial salute" from the fireworks pile and dropped it into a launch tube. Ron walked over to a box of railroad safety flares, picked one up, pulled off its cap an struck it against the top of the flare which quickly began to burn with a plume of bright red fire. He turned and smiled at Duane, strode to the front of the barge, bent down and pointed the flame at the fuse dangling from the launch tube. The fuse hissed to life and Ron quickly retreated toward the back of the barge.

With a loud thump, the shell rocketed skyward followed by a faint trail of sparks. High above the waiting crowd, the shell burst with a bright flash followed by a thunderclap explosion. At the same instant the aerial bomb exploded, Ron's shoe struck the forgotten protruding nail.

Accidents are almost always connected by a long chain of events; shooting the fireworks over Lake Okabena, an idea for building a floating barge to launch fireworks, using volunteer firemen to build a barge, a clumsy trip, a hammer lost overboard and, worst of all, a nail driven only halfway.

Ron fell forward toward the pile of neatly stacked fireworks. As he fell, the railroad flare flew from his hand and landed atop the pile. Ron jumped up and quickly snatched up the flare. He was fast but not fast enough; a soft hiss and a wisp of smoke rose from the pile.

"FIRE!" Ron yelled as he grabbed for a fire extinguisher. Pulling the pin, he squeezed the handle and directed the spray toward the sparking fuse. Fireworks are designed to be protected from moisture as a measure to prevent misfires from damp fuses so the extinguisher spray did not penetrate quickly enough to staunch the ignition of the propellant charge which exploded with a fiery bang. In an instant the top of the fireworks pile was ablaze.

"JUMP!" Ron called to the launch crew.

There was no thought of the now useless life jackets that sat on the edge of the deck; like a precision diving team, the three men hit the water all at once. As if it was coordinated, a "Peony" display charge went off next creating a bright glittering ball of fiery orange sparks on top of the now blazing pile of fireworks. The Peony was quickly followed by a pair of bright white "Chrysanthemums" that blossomed just above the barge.

Onshore, the viewers marveled at the unusual opening display. Many quickly decided that this would be the most spectacular fireworks show that they'd ever seen. It was! Giant orbs of glowing, sparkling and twinkling colored lights festooned the barge. Whiz-bangs shot skyward and exploded. Shells arched into the water and their colorful lights erupted in geysers of colored fire. Mostly the fireworks pile just seethed, burned and erupted with geysers of brilliantly colored sparks and thundered loudly as shells exploded.

With the flat calm over the lake, the smoke from the exploding pyrotechnics now completely enveloped the barge and each fiery eruption released what looked like colored lightning in the smoky cloud.

Cliff Nelson was sitting in the cabin of the dredge workboat "Okabena," smoking a cigarette and watching the men on the barge when he saw Ron stumble and the flare arc toward the fireworks pile and the first explosion and the three workers diving into the lake. Without hesitation, Cliff flicked his cigarette into the lake, started the workboat engine and leapt onto pump house platform to untie the boat. Once free, Cliff started slowly guiding the boat into the lake bent on rescuing the swimmers. In the short time it took to get underway the barge had disappeared in the cloud of smoke from the exploding shells and only the flashes of light pointed the way to the barge. Cliff put the boat engine in reverse and backed toward the power plant water intake platform. Two volunteer firemen standing helplessly by their truck saw Cliff returning and ran down to the platform. As the boat drew close they jumped aboard and Cliff shifted into forward gear, gunned the engine and headed back into the lake.

"Lay down on the bow and signal me if you see one of the guys." Cliff was now aware that there were exploding shells flying everywhere and knew he couldn't get too close without running the risk of getting burned or setting the boat on fire.

Ron Caswell started to swim away from the barge and then realized that the smoke obscured the shore and he didn't know which direction to swim. He wished he'd put on a life jacket so he could just relax and float until things quieted down. Even with the flashes of light from the exploding fireworks it was now growing dark and beneath the layer of smoke the water was completely black. Treading water, Ron was now becoming tense with anxiety.

Cliff turned on the boat's running lights and then searched the dim cockpit for a flashlight. He found one, turned it on and called to one of the men laying down on the bow. "Take the light and shine it on the water to see if you can spot anyone. I'll cut the engine so you can hear any calls." Cliff gunned the engine momentarily to give the boat some forward momentum and then switched it off, letting the boat glide toward the barge. The explosions had slowed and few flashes and the faint glow from the fire on the smoke shrouded barge told Cliff where to point the boat.

Ron heard a boat engine surge and then stop. "Over here. I'm over here!" He yelled as loudly as he could.

Cliff caught the faint sound of a voice off to his right. Starting the engine, he steered toward the sound, gunned the engine and quickly shut it off again and drifted forward.

Ron yelled again. "I'm right ahead of you." Now the flashlight silhouetted him and the boat crew caught sight of his waving arms.

As they pulled Ron over the side of the boat, Cliff asked where the other two were.

"We all jumped and I don't know where Duane and Fred ended up. Nobody said anything; we just jumped."

The explosion of multicolored flame and the booms of detonating powder charges stunned the watching crowd. Mouths agape they could only watch, transfixed by the noise, smoke and chaos of the violent maelstrom of flashing lights and explosions. It seemed longer but it took only two and a half minutes for all two hundred shells to explode. Soon, only silence and a cloud of smoke remained. No one on shore moved or spoke.

The spell was broken by the loud and long honk of a car horn; then someone cheered, then hundreds of others seated in their cars joined into a joyful cacophony of discordant car horn blasts. The crowd on shore quickly broke into wild cheers and waved with both relief and joy. What seemed to be disaster had now been transformed into a unique and exciting entertainment!

Cliff heard to horn honking and cheering as he steered the Okabena through the smoke toward the faint orange glow of the burning barge. As he drew near, Fred Richie's voice echoed out from underneath the barge. Fred was quickly pulled aboard.

"Did you see Duane?" Panic now crept into Cliff's voice. "We need to find Duane!"

When Ron yelled "JUMP," Duane was standing next to the pile of life jackets. He turned and grabbed one as he leapt off the barge. He pulled on the life jacket and started to swim away from the barge as fireworks flew into the water around him and erupted with booms and bursts of flaming sparks. Confused, Duane began to swim away faster without any idea which way he was headed. By now the pall of smoke obscured nearly everything leaving Duane directionless. He kept swimming and finally caught a glimpse of a white light on the masthead of a nearby boat.

On a whim, Brad Dickey took some left-over bunting used to decorate the family drug store and decked out the family runabout. He borrowed his Dad's World War II army uniform jacket and cap and joined the boat parade. When the parade ended, Brad just cut the engine on the boat and turned on the white masthead light and drifted on the flat calm lake, waiting for the twilight to deepen enough for the fireworks to start. Like nearly everyone else, Brad had been transfixed by the violent explosions that erupted from the barge as the display went terribly awry. Thinking there must be some way to help; he started the boat engine and headed for the barge. He slowed as the smoke cloud expanded toward him and fireworks began flying around him, exploding overhead and on the water. As he started to turn away he spotted the silhouette of a swimmer emerging from the smoke and waving a hand. Brad turned the boat toward Duane and shut off the engine. When Duane grabbed the side of the boat, Brad leaned way over the far side to keep from tipping over.

"Can you get a leg over the side?"

Duane swung a leg out of the water and over the edge of the boat.

"Now just roll yourself in."

Duane quickly heaved himself over the side of the boat and dropped to the bottom with a squish.

"Thanks for the lift. The water wasn't too bad but I was afraid my shoes would come off before someone found me." Duane gave a wan smile and shook his head.

Brad took Duane to the power plant water intake platform, dropped him off and headed back into the lake, swung around the smoke cloud and headed toward the city boat house.

Cliff guided the Okabena along the edge of the smoke cloud, slowly circling the smoldering barge looking for any sign of Duane. Brad spotted the Okabena and guessed they were looking for barge crew members. He pulled alongside and explained to Cliff that Duane was safely onshore.

Its life saving effort ended, the Okabena ferried a couple of volunteer firemen out to the barge where they quickly doused the burning planks, then pulled up the anchors and the workboat finished its day towing the barge off the lake to be tied it up at the water intake platform.

The crowd drifted away and the volunteer firemen plus a few onlookers walked the two blocks to Ray's Café and drank a few glasses of beer to decompress. The Fourth of July Celebration came to an end.

No one remembers the event and even members of the fire department have never acknowledged being involved either; my guess is most likely to avoid embarrassment. Only Brad Dickey ever admitted his role and he moved to Alaska long ago and can now no longer be reached.

The Aerialists

I am a member of the Worthington High School 1956 graduating class; my brother, George, is one year ahead of me, class of '55. For a reason I can't explain, I had many more friends in his class than in my own class and that has some impact on this tale. This shared comradery meant that George and I were often together which created some tension, as brothers are naturally somewhat competitive and there is always the primal urge by the older sibling to kill the younger one because the younger one does stupid things and irritates the older one. We both survived but there were some close calls.

The main benefit to following my older brother was George always blazed the trail and always bore the brunt of missteps, and always took arrows in the back; he was the first to come home with alcohol on his breath, he got the first traffic ticket and so on. I, on the other hand, was the invisible child, the forgotten middle one. Because I was walking in George's footsteps my missteps didn't usually didn't show. Some times that is a very big advantage; this was one of those times.

Two blocks west of our house on West Ninth Avenue, stood Worthington's newest water tower, a fine sturdy structure that rose about one hundred feet above the neighborhood. Most of us didn't pay much attention to this piece of municipal infrastructure but a couple of George's classmates were attracted to the structure's gracefully rounded, pumpkin-shaped tank; viewing it as a blank canvas waiting for them to create an artistic statement or at least to publicize their future matriculation from Worthington's school system.

On a warm summer night, these two aerial artists found a way to defeat the security device meant to deter young men bent on scaling to the top walkway that surrounded the tower's tank. Once elevated, they set to work with the can of green paint and paint brushes that they brought up with them. Unnoticed and undetected they proceeded to emblazon the side of the tank with the mark of their tribe, "CLASS OF 55," in bright, green paint.

This act of defacing a public structure didn't cause much of a stir in the general population. We noticed it. We criticized the somewhat hap-hazard technique and dismissed the effort as very minimal due to the small size of the letters. Most of my friends, members of the identified class, averred that they could do better and set about looking for a new canvas on which they could display their artistic prowess. While I was privy to these discussions, my membership in the inferior class of `56 meant that I was viewed as only an onlooker and not permitted a voice or vote on any of the plans as they hatched. Hatching didn't take long.

The paint was barely dry on the Worthington tank when George and his friends put their plan into action. This team was quickly expanded by the addition of the two original artists. With a larger group, the plan was broadened into a "double" -paint two towers on the same night. The neighboring towns of Heron Lake and Okabena were selected as targets; both had towers that were deemed climbable.

Heron Lake, about sixteen miles northeast of Worthington on highway 60, is a modest city with a population then of about 900. The most prominent structure in Heron Lake is the twin steepled Sacred Heart Catholic Church. The Heron Lake tower was almost in the center of town, two blocks west of Sacred Heart, so there was some risk that the climbers would be discovered and thwarted. They were brave and foolish so they didn't care.

Okabena is about 6 miles south east of Heron Lake and had just completed a brand new water system that featured a sparkling new tower; quite a feat for a town with a population of just under 300. Their new tower was on the south edge of town and seemed an easy target.

The team was divided up. Brad had a bigger car; a 1930's something Dodge four-door, so he was selected to transport the Heron Lake unit. As he had the room, I was permitted to ride is his car. LaVoy barrowed his mother's car, a 1939 Chevy and he led the Okabena unit. Jon contributed the green paint and a number of brushes, courtesy of his father's hardware store.

On the appointed night we hung around Worthington; waiting impatiently for it to get late enough so everyone would be off the streets and in bed. At about 11 we set off. Matt, Roger, George and I rode in Brad's car. Bill, Jon and Marc rode with LaVoy. Okabena is farther away than Heron Lake so we didn't expect to see LaVoy's until the next day. The Brad team was pretty keyed up and the trip to Heron Lake was a circus as we all jumped around in the car, making a lot of racket and pestering each other.

Brad finally slowed down on the outskirts of Heron Lake and we crept quietly into town. The only place to park was on the street right next to the tower. Brad stopped the car; I got out and checked to make sure the coast was clear. Someone followed me out and slammed the car door which brought several muttered admonitions to be quiet. With everyone out of the car, Matt and Roger grabbed the paint and a couple of brushes and strode to the tower. Roger gave Matt a boost up to the first rung of the ladder. As soon as Matt started his climb, Roger jumped up and grabbed the bottom rung and followed Matt up. It is important to note that Roger is a natural athlete, slim, trim, supple and strong; whereas Matt is a studious lad, big, blocky and relatively unathletic. Their progress was uncoordinated and noisy; Matt's heavy footsteps clanged loudly on the metal rungs of the ladder and Roger exhorted him to be quieter; in whispers loud enough to be heard blocks away. Reaching the platform at top of the ladder, their route was blocked by a second ladder which led from the walkway around the tower up the side of the tank. The second ladder swiveled sideways and the only way onto the platform was to move that ladder off to one side. Matt grabbed ahold and started to pull the ladder sideways causing a very loud metallic squeak. Everyone froze expecting lights to come on and people to appear. Nothing moved. Matt grunted and mumbled something to Roger. Roger cursed and began to climb down.

"I'm stuck," Matt hissed.

Roger stopped and began to climb back up. When he reached Matt there was more mumbling and the sounds of a struggle and a loud rip. Finally, the two began to descend. Roger dropped to the ground followed by Matt. Roger jumped to his feet, grabbed a rung and began to climb back up. Matt sat in a heap below the ladder.

"I think I ripped my shirt." Matt stood up and held out the two brushes he was carrying.

Meanwhile, the Okabena unit wasn't faring so well either. As they wheeled into town and approached the Okabena water tower they could see that something was amiss. Instead of finding a dark and quiet field on the edge of town they came upon a small crowd gathered around the tower, enjoying some sort of late-night party. It was quickly obvious that they'd have to abandon any thought of climbing and painting in Okabena. The decision was made to head for Heron Lake and join our effort.

LaVoy drove north only a couple of miles before Jon complained of excessive bladder pressure. LaVoy slowed, pulled into what turned out to be the driveway to a one-room country schoolhouse. While Jon relieved himself, Marc and LaVoy surveyed the beautiful, blank white wall facing the highway on the west side of school house. Their artistic fervor, unrequited by the failure in Okabena, took over. They grabbed the paint and proceeded to swiftly emblazon the white wall with "WHS CLASS OF `55." With that accomplished, the quartet jumped back in the car and raced toward Heron Lake.

"Car!" I whispered loudly and ducked behind the Dodge. As the car rounded the corner towards us, its lights blinked off and it coasted to a stop behind our car. It was LaVoy's Okabena unit.

Jon hopped out and slid up next to me. "Are you guys about done?"

I shook my head and pointed up. "Matt got stuck trying to get on the platform and had to climb back down."

Once George saw the paint brushes, he grabbed them from Matt, jumped up to the ladder and climbed up to helped Roger. Brad headed up right behind George. By now the noises from the tower had subsided and we relaxed a little. The Okabena unit lit cigarettes and watched. Matt got in Brad's car and sulked.

"Heads up," George whispered loudly as he leaned over the tower railing and dropped the wet paint brushes.

As Roger, Brad and George started down we all clambered into the cars and got ready for our get-away. The three painters jumped in and we headed quickly out of town and back toward Worthington.

Two days later George and I with a bunch of other Explorer Scouts got on a Chicago and Northwestern train to St. Paul, heading north for Ely and a two-week Boundary Waters Wilderness Canoe trip into the Quetico Provincial Park in Canada. The first stop on the Worthington to St. Paul leg was Heron Lake. Nearing Heron Lake, we peered out the window as the train slowed; waiting for the first glimpse of our aerial art work. As the tower came into view we were surprised by a shiny silver rectangle covering the area George, Roger and Brad had painted.

"That was quick. I wanted to see how we did." George looked at me and shook his head dejectedly. That quick paint-over job should have been a signal that something was up but we didn't catch it.

Two weeks in the Canadian wilderness was wonderful. I don't think we thought about Worthington or water towers the whole time we paddled, camped, cooked, fished and enjoyed our carefree wilderness experience. We finally started the long train trek home.

Mom and Dad met us when our train arrived in Worthington. We were greeted warmly but both George and I sensed some stress as we loaded our gear in the car. Our folks were pretty quiet on the drive home; that wasn't a good sign. After we brought the luggage into the house, Mom and Dad sat down at the kitchen table.

"Have a seat," said Dad.

We sat down at the table.

"Read this," Dad handed a letter to George.

George's face turned white and his eyes widened. The letter was from Nobles County Sheriff Sandy Deuel, now George understood why Mom and Dad seemed stressed. The letter was a summons for George and his parents to appear in Judge Vincent Hollaren's court in the matter of criminal trespass and defacing public property in Jackson County, Minnesota; the towns of Heron Lake and Okabena were in Jackson County.

Explaining that we'd been water tower painting eased the tension somewhat but going for a visit to Judge Hollaren probably wasn't going to end well. We stayed home, washed our dirty clothes and put away our camping gear. George called Matt and learned that all of the participants would be going to court tomorrow. I was left out which was good and bad. Since I hadn't climbed or painted I wouldn't face any punishment. At the same time, I wanted to be there to see what was actually going to happen.

Morning came. Mom, Dad and George drove off leaving me and my younger brother, Tom, to fend for ourselves. I think I felt guilty and mowed the lawn for penance. Time dragged by slowly but at last I saw our big Dodge coming down the street.

George got out first; a slight smile on his face. Mom and Dad were relaxed so I guess George wasn't going to jail.

"This isn't a laughing matter." Dad looked at Mom.

"If you say so. I guess it turned out to be just a lesson for everyone."

I could hardly wait to find out what happened. We all went inside for lunch and the story spilled out. On the day George and I left on the canoe trip, Roger and Brad showed up at Max Shapiro's junk yard with some scrap steel and copper they found. Max bought it. There had been a rash of pilferage from construction sites around the area so Sheriff Deuel had asked Max to be on the lookout for suspicious scrap sales. Max dutifully reported Brad and Roger. That day the sheriff contacted both boys, invited them to his office for an inquiry into the scrap they sold Max. During his questioning, he noted that both boys had a lot of green paint on their hands.

The green paint might have passed unnoticed but for the Heron Lake water tower. Unlike the Worthington tower and the Okabena school house, the painters choose to use the Worthington High School sports teams' name, "TROJANS," on that tower; a seemingly unremarkable substitution. Unknowingly they had ignited a firestorm of indignation.

Some members of the Heron Lake community interpreted the name as an advertisement for a popular brand of male contraceptives; a particularly egregious act. The community quickly sprang into action; the offending name was painted over the very next morning. The Jackson County Sheriff was called and immediate action was demanded.

It didn't take long for less emotional heads to determine that the paint job was a prank and not an offensive ad and most likely carried out by those no-good hoodlums from Worthington. They also quickly connected the Okabena school house to the same gang.

Since everything was painted green; it's easy to see why Sheriff Deuel was quick to connect Roger and Brad to paint job. They were more or less caught "green handed!"

In spite of the angst in Jackson County, the boys, being juveniles, the matter was dealt with in Nobles County and in Judge Hollaren's Juvenile court.

It's not that the Judge was particularly harsh; it was rather that the normal mode of punishment for delinquent deeds meant handing over your driver's license for at least 30 days and even longer for non-traffic stunts like shoplifting or fighting in public. While juvenile delinquents were never publically identified; walking when you should be driving quickly flagged you as having visited the good judge for some misdeed. It was like being branded with a big red D for Delinquent!

So it came to the seven lads sitting nervously in the courtroom, flanked by their parents. While it was embarrassing being in court with your beloved child, it was made somewhat worse being there with so many other adults who now knew that your son was a delinquent. The tension was eased by the fact that their sons belonged to the same crowd!

Testimony began with a recitation of the evil acts. LaVoy and Jon described how they came to paint an innocent schoolhouse due to Jon's need of relief. Their description was graphic but also mildly amusing as both Jon and LaVoy were quick witted and glib. They set the stage for what came next.

Brad told of driving into Heron Lake and parking the car. Roger described boosting Matt up to the ladder and climbing up behind him. At this point Matt interrupted and told that he'd never gotten up on the tower so he was innocent and should be absolved of any illegal conduct. The judge asked for an explanation of why Matt climbed but didn't actually get to the top.

Matt said his shirt got caught and he got stuck. Roger then described the struggle to get Matt unstuck. As Roger warmed to the rhetoric of his testimony he managed to blurt out that Matt's "fat ass" was too big to fit through the opening. The seriousness of the proceeding had now been fatally damaged and the judge moved quickly on to the more mundane business of meting out the punishments.

The miscreants stood and faced Judge Hollaren, heads bowed humbly. The judge's first act was to ask each one of them to hand over their driver's licenses. They stepped forward one at a time and offered them up. Once he had all of licenses, the judge pulled open a desk drawer, withdrew a large manila envelope, dropped the licenses in with exaggerated deliberation, licked the flap, sealed it, put the envelope in the drawer and pushed the drawer shut with a flourish akin to a hangman pulling the lever on a gallows trapdoor. Next the judge called out each of the boys.

LaVoy and Jon were required to buy enough white paint to cover their work on the Okabena schoolhouse (two coats if necessary!). Then all four members of the Okabena unit were ordered to repaint the schoolhouse wall.

Roger, Brad and my brother were each fined $50 for "defacing public property" and Matt was fined $45 for attempting.

Later on, one of the boys was overheard saying Matt got $5 off for having a big butt. Everyone laughed. As far as I know, we never did any painting like that again.

High Jinks

We may have abandoned paint but we hadn't quite abandoned mischief. I started my last year at Worthington High and fall was advancing with darkness coming earlier each day. On a Thursday night in late October; looking for something to do, I wandered down to Emil's Pool Hall. LaVoy was there sitting on a stool watching the players disinterestedly and looking bored until he looked up, saw me and smiled.

"What's up?"

"Nothing's up Clam. What's up with you?"

LaVoy's nickname, Clam, had a long history connected to his adamant refusal to ever admit to anything. As a young boy he had trouble dealing with authority and often failed to follow instructions or obey orders which inevitably led to confrontations. When pressed, he simply "clammed up." He was older now, undoubtedly wiser but still just as stubborn.

"Well, I've been thinking about school," LaVoy looked at me and smiled. "I got there early on Monday and watched Art put up the flag."

Art Gustafson is the head custodian at the high school. Every school day around seven a.m. he'd walk out the front entrance and down the wide front walkway to the flagpole in the center of the courtyard. Art carried an American Flag which he attached to the lanyard looping down the pole and quickly hoisted the flag up; a pretty simple process that hardly anyone paid any attention to; except LaVoy that morning.

"I wondered what he'd do if the rope got stuck up at the top and he couldn't raise the flag. How can you unstick something that high up?"

I suppose I've thought of that problem a time or two but only briefly. I looked at LaVoy and waited to see where his question was going. I didn't have to wait long to find out.

"I think we should go over to the school and check out the flag pole." LaVoy hopped off his perch and headed for the door.

I scrambled after him and we ran up the stairs to the street, ducked down the alley and headed for LaVoy's house.

"Let's borrow Mom's car." LaVoy's mother generously and foolishly always let LaVoy use her car. When we rode with him we always chipped in a few bucks and bought enough gas to bring the car back with more gas that we burned. It worked well enough and LaVoy's mother never turned him down.

"Let's see if Matt's home." LaVoy started the car, turned down the alley and headed down Tenth Street toward Matt's house.

We picked up Matt and headed toward the high school while LaVoy told Matt of his scientific quest to discover what happened when the rope got stuck at the top of flag pole. Matt was willing to participate in this exciting voyage of discovery. I'll admit that I didn't quite know exactly what we were going to do and I'm not sure LaVoy did either.

We parked directly across from the school entrance; which was also directly across from the flag pole. The street was dark and neighborhood quiet. There didn't seem to be anything going on at the school; it too was dark and quiet, so we got out of the car and strode casually over to the flag pole and surrounded it. We examined it closely. The rope was wound around a cleat bolted to the pole and the two clips used to secure the flag were spliced into the one strand of the rope. As we stood there examining the pole and contemplating the next move, LaVoy turned away and walked over to the curb, stopping in front of a "NO PARKING" sign bolted to a stout wooden post.

"I wonder if we can pull this up?" LaVoy reached out, wrapping his arms around the wooden post that held the sign. Small of stature but well-muscled with thick, strong legs he wrapped his arms around the post, looked back at us and grinned. Bending his knees, LaVoy lifted upwards, pulling on the post. The post didn't budge. He stepped back, grabbed the post and began to rock it back and forth; gradually gaining movement and loosening the post. LaVoy again bent his knees, wrapped his arms around the post and strained upwards. This time the post slid out of the hole.

"Nice work. What are you going to do with that?" Matt walked over to LaVoy, grabbing the end of the post.

LaVoy smiled and pointed up. "We're going to hoist this puppy up the pole just like a flag."

That seemed like a good idea. Then we pondered the next part of the problem, how to do it so that Art couldn't just pull the post back down. We quickly determined that we'd need some sort of slip-knot at we could pull tight when the post reached the top of the pole. We tried a few knots without much success. It took us a while but we finally found the right combination and hoisted the signpost up to the top of the pole and snubbed the knot tight. The post and sign dangled awkwardly at the top and no tugging was going to bring it back down. We left, satisfied with our ingenuity and eager to get back to school early enough on Friday to watch Art when he discovered our handiwork.

I got up earlier than usual the next morning and arrived at school before seven. I went in a side door and strait up to a classroom that overlooked the courtyard. The post swung idly atop the flag pole and Art was nowhere to be seen. Before long the bells rang and I left the window and headed for my first class. At lunchtime I headed out the front door and spotted LaVoy leaning against the Veteran's Memorial in front of the school's main entrance.

"No Art," I said.

"They're probably trying to figure out how to get it down. Pretty high up to use a ladder. I hope we're around to see how they do it." LaVoy walked over to the pole and looked up.

The school cafeteria was in the basement of Central Grade School two blocks away and most students going to lunch at the cafeteria left the high school building through the main front door hurried down the sidewalk and under the flag pole. LaVoy and I stood there and watched them stream by; no one even looked up. We waited a few minutes and then joined the procession.

It took two days before the post was removed from the flag pole. Alas, no one seems to have witnessed the process used to get the post down. They must have waited until Saturday when no one was around the school. One rumor that seemed credible was that the local power company boys rigged up a ladder system that reached high enough and found somebody brave enough to climb up and undo the slip knot. We did notice that they'd installed a new rope and had added a security system. The snaps were now spliced into the rope so they couldn't be removed. One of the snaps had a ring welded to it and there was a similar ring welded to the cleat on the pole. A large padlock now anchored the two rings together. We'd never get another chance.

Within two years the old school was replaced by a new, modern one on Clary Street where the county fairgrounds once stood. The truncated obelisk with the Veterans Memorial Plaque survives and is located just off Clary Street right at the front entrance of the new high school. If you look closely, you'll see a tall slender flagpole just to the left of the new school's front doors. I wonder if it too came from the old campus and was moved and if they still padlock the rope to keep mischief makers at bay?

The old Senior High School, used for junior high classes after 1958. Eventually demolished. Photo courtesy Nobles County Historical Society

Time Line

This is a confession of sorts. I've never told anyone and never really expected that someday I could tell this tale of what happened to me so long ago. It all began on Tuesday, June 15, 1956. I was going to be eighteen in two months and had graduated from high school on May 31, just two weeks before. On that May Day, all 157 members of Worthington High School's Class of '56 crowded on the stage at the Memorial Auditorium, sweated through a forgettable commencement address about the world of tomorrow by some guy named Furbay from Transworld Airlines, grabbed our diplomas and rushed for the exits. Someone took a picture with Dad's camera as I stood between Mom and Dad on the auditorium steps looking somewhat bookish in my cap and gown. Mom hugged and kissed me and Dad shook my hand. We may have talked but I don't remember anything after the handshake.

My girlfriend, Barbara Mahoney, and I had planned to go to a graduation party after commencement at

Patsy Albinson's house. It would be a grand party and I'd been excited that Patsy had invited the two of us. The day before graduation Barbara called me and told me she wasn't going to the party with me and that she wouldn't be seeing me anymore either. My world went black. The excitement of graduation was gone, obliterated by despair and sadness. I knew there was nothing I could do, no way to bring Barbara back so I went over to the Patsy's house anyway, said hello to the crowd and slunk away into the dark to brood over my fate. I was young enough to recover and that recovery was helped along by the story I'm going to tell at last.

A few days ago I got a letter announcing the 60th reunion of the Worthington High School Class of 1956. Along with the invitation was a list of class members who've "gone on ahead." I saw Barbara's name on the list. They're all dead now I thought; Barbara, Rosemary Simons, Tacy Vanzwol, Ellen Williams and Jim Rossberg. As far as I know, Barbara never told anyone about what happened that night, at least no one ever mentioned anything about it and now I guess the story can be told.

The summer of graduation I was working at the Oxford Standard Station on the west edge of Worthington. Interstate 90 didn't exist then so highway 16 was the main tourist route across southern Minnesota; a steady stream of cars heading west and east and going right past the station. We were usually pretty busy pumping gas, fixing tires and selling radiator bug screens. The station opened at 7 AM and closed by 10 PM. I usually opened up 4 mornings a week and closed up 5 times a week. I was saving money for college so working long hours was ok by me and kept my mind off Barbara.

The sun had set on July 15th and by about 10 o'clock only the last glow of twilight remained; I was standing in the doorway at the station getting ready to shut off the gas pumps and turn off the outside lights when the Mahoney's folk's big black Buick pulled onto the apron with Barbara behind the wheel. As the car stopped, Barb's head dropped between her arms as she slumped over the steering wheel. I stepped outside and walked toward the car. Barbara didn't stir. I hesitated, waiting for Barb to make the first move and when she stayed still, I reached down and opened the car door. Barb raised her head slightly and turned toward me; her face was wet with tears and ashen with fright.

"Help me," she sobbed.

I didn't know what to say so I just held out my hand, took her arm and pulled her out of the car and guided her to the bench in front of the station building, sat her down and sat down next to her.

"What's wrong?"

"He was grabbing me and I hit him." She inhaled slowly, sank forward and put her hands over her face.

I reached up and pulled a hand away from her face. With the other hand still covering half her face she stared at me with the one tearful eye. I didn't have the faintest idea what she was talking about.

Then she blurted out, "I killed him." She whispered "He's in the back seat."

I didn't understand what she was saying. The idea of her killing someone didn't register clearly. All I could do was to blurt out; "I'll call the police."

"No! No! I didn't mean to do it. Everyone will know. Won't you help me?"

I recovered a bit and actually began to understand what she was saying.

"Ok, tell me exactly what happened."

It never occurred to me to look in the back seat of her car to see if there really was a dead body. I needed to get her to calm down and then try to convince her to go the police. So I asked her to start at the beginning and tell me what happened.

Barbara, Rosemary, Tacy and Ellen were at the band concert at Chautauqua Park she said. It was so hot they decided to leave ahead of the crowd and go to Pratt's Ice Cream Parlor for an ice cream cone. Barb was driving her Dad's car and Tacy her own car. Someone suggested going to the drive-in theater. When they arrived at Pratt's there was almost nobody inside. The only ones they recognized were classmates, Mike Thompson and Lois Nau. Lois sometimes worked nights a Pratt's; her boyfriend, Leon Weise was in the army so she was ok working nights. None of the four girls liked Mike so they just ignored him.

Barb ordered an ice cream cone and was paying for it when Tacy said she had decided to just go home, it was too hot to go to the drive-in. Rosemary and Ellen agreed and said they were calling it a night too. Barbara told me she was a little ticked off but didn't much care except she didn't want to be left alone at Pratt's with Mike Thompson. As the four girls walked outside, Barb said she was going to drive around Lake Okabena to Slater Park, eat her cone and watch the sunset.

"Mike must have overheard me telling everyone where I was going. I drove out there, parked along the lake, got out and sat on the front fender, the sun was almost down, it was very still. I was just finishing my ice cream when Mike drove in behind me."

Mike had a reputation as rough guy and he ran around with a rough bunch that was avoided by the saddle shoe crowd, which included Barb and her friends. Barb said she was afraid of him.

Mike got out of his car and walked over to Barb, hopping up on the fender next to her. Feeling trapped, Barb didn't move and Mike did all the talking; asking her if she was still going out with me and wondering if she'd like to go out with him. Barb said she just shook her head. Then he put his arm around her. She tried to pull away but he held her tight. He slid his free hand up her dress along her thigh. She struggled and pushed his hand but he was too strong. Then he jumped off the fender, pulling her with him and pushed her to the back of her car. He jerked the back door open and pushed her onto the back seat and fell on top of her.

"I don't know why I didn't scream. I was paralyzed, I couldn't think, I just wanted him to stop."

She described wrestling him as he tore at her clothes and pulled down her patties. Somehow he let go of an arm and she reached out to hit him. When her hand touched the floor by the back seat, she felt something hard, grabbed it and swung as hard as she could.

"He went limp. I pushed him off and pulled myself out of the car. Then I started hitting him with my fists but he didn't move at all. My dad plays horse shoes in a league and I'd grabbed one of his horse shoes from the floor of the back seat and that's what I hit Mike with. I didn't mean to kill him. I just wanted to run, so I drove the rest of the way around the lake. Will you help me?"

"Barbara, we've got to call the police otherwise you'll be in even more trouble." I was sure she'd make things worse by trying to avoid being found out.

Barb was convinced that I'd be able to get her out of this fix and nobody would ever know. I don't know if I was feeling sorry for Barb or sorry for me; anyway, she got me to agree to help her and to get Mike's body out of her car. The gas station had two service bays so I drove the big black Buick into one and then drove my car into the other one and then pulled the shop doors closed. The shop lights were off leaving the service bays dark and the outside lights reflecting off the glass doors would stop prying eyes from seeing what I was doing. I opened the back door of the Buick and pulled Mike's body out. Now all I had to do was get him into trunk of my '39 Ford Coupe. Mike wasn't too big but trying to lift and move a dead body isn't really a one-man job. I pulled, pushed and rolled until I got his head and arms over the bumper and into the trunk. Then I was able to lift his legs up enough to roll him into the trunk and get the lid closed. I was really sweating by the time I was done. I opened one service bay door and backed the Buick out, parking in the same spot where Barb stopped when she drove in. I was relieved that no customers stopped while I was wrestling with Mike.

Barb was still sitting on the bench where I left her. I went in the station and bought a bottle of Nesbit's Orange from the pop machine, brought it out and handed it to her. She took a drink of the pop and smiled weakly at me. I sat down next to her, took her hand and shook my head.

"Barb, listen to me very carefully, what I'm going to tell you is really important because we're about to do something that could get us both big trouble if we're ever found out." She nodded and took another sip of the orange pop.

"First, you've got to promise to never, ever tell anyone what you did tonight. No ifs, ands, or buts; do you understand? No friends, no parents, no boyfriend, no one you think can keep a secret. Can you do that?"

She looked at me and nodded.

"If anyone asks about tonight, you have to tell exactly what you did tonight; just leave out what happened with Mike. Otherwise, don't ever change a single detail. Don't ever leave anything out. Don't ever make anything up; always tell the exact truth. Do you understand?" I let go of her hand and squeezed her shoulder.

"Yes. I'll never, ever tell and I'll never let on that you helped me."

"There's one more thing you've got to make sure you get right." I paused to emphasize the importance to my question.

"Why did you come here to see me?" I knew that if anyone ever followed her path it would lead them here and she needed a good answer to that question. I guess

I needed that answer too; she'd dumped me but came running as soon as she needed help.

"This part is true," she said. "I've feel bad about what I did to you and the way I broke it off. I didn't have the nerve to see you face to face but I want to say I'm sorry for the way things worked out. Before Mike drove up, while I was eating my ice cream cone and watching the sunset, I decided that I'd see if you were working tonight and come over and face you and apologize. So that's the reason I came to you." She looked away for a moment and then stood up.

"What will you do with Mike?"

I said I hadn't figured that out yet but not to worry. I actually came up with a plan while I was putting Mike in the trunk of my car but I wouldn't tell Barb, she mustn't ever know what I did so she could never slip up and get me dragged in.

"Go home. Tell your folks you stopped to see me and you're feeling too low to talk. Take a bath and go to bed." I took her hand and walked her to the car. She squeezed my hand, got in her car, started it and drove away without looking back. I didn't know it then but that was the last time I'd ever talk to her. We showed up at the same place from time-to-time, even said hello but we never actually talked beyond the hello and how are you. For some reason she never ever came to our high school class reunions even though she lived in St. Paul.

I turned off the lights outside the station; made sure the electricity was turned off to the gas pumps, took the money drawer out of the cash register and hid it under the pop machine, went into the service bay and grabbed a bundle of shop towels and threw them on the front seat of my car, opened the service bay door, got in my car and backed it out of the service bay, pulled the door down, locked the front door of the station, got in my car and headed east down Oxford Street.

Worthington grew fast after the war, forcing the city to build a new sewage treatment plant just east of town. The plant included two large treatment ponds surrounded by a chain link fence. A gravel track wound around the ponds with a locked gate at the far end. The ponds were far enough out of town that they were completely hidden by farm fields and tall weeds grew up on both sides of the track, tall enough to keep a car hidden. The summer before a few of us got a six pack of beer and decided that parking on that gravel track would be a good spot to avoid being caught while we sipped that forbidden brew. We broke the padlock on the gate and drove in by the ponds. Once we were next to the water, the smell was too much so we left and never came back. So that's where I headed; I was pretty sure I could drop Mike off there without being seen.

I turned off Oxford Street unto the gravel road leading to the treatment plant. Once I'd gone a short distance I shut off my headlights, the rising moon gave me just enough light to see the road. When I spotted the gate I stopped the car by pulling the hand brake so my brake lights wouldn't go on. I shut off the engine, rolled down my window and sat for a few seconds. Nothing was stirring, totally quiet; no cars coming. I jumped out, ran to the trunk, opened it, pulled out the handle to my tire jack, closed the trunk lid and walked to the gate. I was going to use the jack handle to pry off the lock. When I reached for the padlock, I discovered that it had been pried open already. It could have been from our break in a year earlier!

I pulled the gate open and sprinted back to my car started it and drove onto the track. I stopped inside the gate, using the hand brake again; got out and closed the gate. I drove in far enough so my car wouldn't be visible from the road. I didn't use the hand brake but just shut off the motor and let the car coast to a stop. I undressed completely, socks, underwear, everything I had on. Leaving my clothes on the seat, I got out, closed the car door with just a soft click. Standing naked next to a sewage treatment pond in the middle of the night is a memory that still makes me shiver but I didn't have time that night to stand out there in the dark naked and shivering.

I opened the trunk and pulled Mike's body out. Then I dragged him off the track and into the pond. At night the water seemed black as ink. The bottom was soft so I sank in as I pulled Mike out toward the middle of the pond. I kept wading out until I was waist deep then I let go of Mike. His body didn't really sink; it floated just beneath the surface. I waded back to the edge of the pond where the banks where lined with large rocks. I picked one that I could carry and waded back toward Mike. I had some trouble finding him in the dark water but I finally bumped into a leg. I slipped the large rock under his shirt so it would stay on his chest and was glad to see him sink out of sight.

I waded back to the car, took the shop towels out and wiped myself off until I was completely dry. I threw the towels in the trunk, got dressed, started the car and backed slowly toward the gate. I opened the gate and backed onto the road. Leaving the car running, I ran to the gate, closed it, made sure the padlock was in a position so it looked like the gate was still locked, and ran back to the car a drove away. I didn't turn the headlights on until I was close to the edge of town.

I got home about 11:30; Mom and Dad were in bed asleep. I decided that I smelled bad enough that I'd better take a shower. If I woke folks up I'd tell them I spilled some gasoline in myself and need to clean off. They didn't wake up.

Worthington was quiet for a couple of days. An abandoned car at a city park took a few days to generate much excitement. We sometimes left our cars to go somewhere with friends and them couldn't remember where we'd left the car. Sometimes it took over a day for us to find the missing vehicle. So it was two days before Mike's car attracted attention and his parents were contacted and people started to wonder where Mike had disappeared to. The police and sheriff departments started a search. The volunteer fire department began dragging Lake Okabena around Slater Park. On the third day, the Worthington Daily Globe headlines proclaimed "SEARCH FOR MISSING WHS GRAD UNDERWAY." The effort was intense but fruitless. The dragging stopped after 4 days. A couple of Boy Scout troops spent a week searching the shoreline for a mile in each direction from the park but didn't turn up anything. The Globe printed an appeal for anyone who had seen anything or had seen Mike on the day he disappeared to contact the sheriff's department. I later learned that Lois Nau was the only one to call.

Jim Rossberg was 4 years ahead of me in school. I think he went to Worthington Junior College for 2 years and then went to work for Sheriff Sandy Deuel as a deputy. Jim was a bright guy and a hard worker and, as the newest member of the department, he was given jobs no one really wanted to do. They gave him the task of gathering information on the disappearance of Mike Thompson.

A week after Mike disappeared; I was cleaning the windshield of a car I'd just filled up when a sheriff's car pulled into the station. I finished with windshield and went inside to ring up the sale.

Jim got out of the squad car and walked inside right behind me. I gave the customer his change and turned to Jim.

"Are you Gary Walters?" I think Jim knew who I was; he really got into being a deputy.

"Yes," I answered trying not to sound nervous.

"I'm investigating Mike Thompson's disappearance and your name came up."

"Me? I haven't seen Mike since the night we graduated.

"Did Barbara Mahoney stop by here to see you around 10 o'clock last Tuesday?"

I took a deep breath and tried to hide my nervousness by looking thoughtful. "Yes, I was getting ready to close up when she drove up."

"Why did she come to see you? What did she want?"

I shook my head and looked down. "We use to go together. We broke up the day before graduation. She said she was feeling bad and wanted to come and apologize. We talked and shared a bottle of pop and then she left." I raised my head and looked him in the eye, hoping I sounded convincing and that Barb and stuck to her story.

Jim asked a few more mostly meaningless questions. I guessed he was checking the time Barb came to the station and when she got there.

Jim said thanks, got in the car and drove away. I hoped that was the end of it.

July faded into August. I worked hard but managed to take a few days off to go swimming at Lake Okoboji in Iowa with LeRoy Nau and Jim Ulrich. I was also getting ready to leave for college at Mankato State. I planned to work right up until the day I left; I need all the money I could save for college.

"BODY FOUND AT SEWAGE PLANT," screamed the headline of Tuesday's Daily Globe. Every Monday, Bill Nyens drove out from the city garage to do a routine check out at the treatment plant. When he finished his work inside the plant he usually drove the track around the ponds to make sure they were draining properly and everything was ok. Monday, August 13th proved to be his unlucky day as he spotted something sticking out above the water in the second pond; tennis shoe with a foot in it! He raced back to the treatment plant, called the city garage, told them what he saw and asked them to call the sheriff. I guess there was quite a stampede to the sewage plant as word spread around town. There didn't seem to be any way they could connect me to the body in the pond so I wasn't worried. Maybe I should have been.

It was a week later to the day when Deputy Rossberg drove up to the station. My boss, Obie O'Brien, was gone making his morning run to the bank so I was alone and we were busy with tourist traffic. Jim parked his car and walked over to the pump island where I was filling up a station wagon loaded with baggage and kids.

"I've got a couple of questions to ask when you get a second." He turned away and walked into the station.

What now I thought. Did Barb blab after they found Mike's body? If she did, my goose was cooked. I finished filling up the station wagon, washed the windows and walked back to the station office where the tourist dad was standing next to the cash register with money in his hand. I rang up the sale, took his cash, counted out his change and pushed the cash drawer closed.

"Can we go back in the shop?" Jim asked as he walked from the office into the service area. Without turning he said, "Where do you keep your shop towels?"

I walked past him and pointed to a cardboard box on the work bench.

"The dirty ones are in a pail next to the bench."

Jim walked over to the box, took one of the towels out and looked at it.

"Who do you get your shop towel service from?"

"United Uniform in Luverne; we get our uniforms from them too." I wondered where this was going to lead.

"Damn." Jim looked at the rag, sighed and then looked at me. "I thought we had a good piece of evidence. They picked up a shop towel by the sewage pond where the body was found. Turns out almost every garage and gas station in town uses United; even the city uses United. Now there's no way to tell where that rag came from. Your towels are even a different color, blue, and the one we found was brown." He handed the towel back to me, turned quickly, walked out, got in his car and left.

If Jim had looked in the dirty towel barrel he'd have discovered it was full of brown towels. The laundry service stopped by every other Monday, picking up our dirty uniforms and shop towels and replacing them with clean ones. Sometimes the bundles of shop towels they left were blue, sometimes brown. The last batch we got were blue, I had escaped suspicion. When drying myself off that night I should have counted the towels I used to make sure I didn't leave one behind; I just picked up the wet ones and threw them in the car trunk and then buried them under dirty towels in the pail the next morning. I must have dropped one and didn't notice it in the dark.

I kept waiting for the other shoe to drop but there no more visits from Rossberg. The Daily Globe ran a story on how Thompson died. When they found the body it was sent to a medical examiner in Minneapolis. Their report said Thompson didn't drown; he was dead before his body went into the pond. The report also said the cause of death was a blow to the base of the skull which fractured his C2 neck vertebra, severing his spinal cord causing him to stop breathing. I think Barb must have grabbed the horseshoe in such a way that she hit him with the pointed open end of the shoe.

After that story there were no more updates on the investigation. I started packing to head for Mankato and the beginning of my college career; thoughts of Mike Thompson and Barb Mahoney had faded.

By the end of August, traffic on Highway 16 slowed and the station wasn't too busy. On late Friday morning, August 31, Obie was in the front office getting a gasoline delivery order ready and I was in the shop mounting a new set of tires. I heard the phone ring but didn't pay much attention, nobody ever called me at the station.

"Gary, it's for you."

I walked into the office puzzled about who would call me at work.

"Is this Gary Walters?" I recognized Jim Rossberg's voice; he was being the deputy again. I told him it was me.

"Can you come down to the Sheriff's office we need to talk?"

My heart sank. Now what turned up? I couldn't think of anything that would drag me back into that sewage pond other than a slip up by Barbara. I told Obie that I was going out for lunch and would finish mounting the tires when I got back. I was pretty nervous on the drive downtown to the courthouse square. As I pulled up to park I looked up at the red brick county jail and sheriff's office. I wondered for a moment if I'd been found out and wouldn't be coming back out. Taking a deep breath I got out of my car and walked up the sheriff's office door, pushed it open and walked in. Jim was sitting at a desk at the back of the room; there was no one else there. He motioned me to a chair next to his desk. I sat down.

"I just got back from a week at the FBI Academy in Arlington, Virginia. Sheriff Deuel sent me to their course in criminal investigation. It was pretty good and I learned a lot." He paused and gazed at me with a self-satisfied smile. "I've worked on this Thompson murder for over a month and never got anywhere. Now I think I've discovered something and I want to go over it with you."

Jim slid a blank sheet of paper over toward me, picked up a pencil and drew a long line across the paper. At the beginning of the line he made a little tic mark and wrote 9:10 under it.

"That's when Barbara and her friends left Pratt's shop. Lois Nau is sure about the time. Barb's friends were also sure about the time.

Now he made another tic mark a little to the right of the first one. He wrote 9:20 under the new tic.

"I drove from Pratt's to Slater Park several times. It never took me more than 8 minutes but we'll be a little generous and give Mahoney 10 minutes."

He then put a little tic mark at the very right end of the line and wrote 9:55 under it.

"Barbara Mahoney got to your station at that time and you've confirmed that. It never took me more than 7 minutes to drive from Slater Park to your gas station but I'll give her a minute or two extra."

He made another tic just to the left of the 9:55 one and wrote 9:45 under it.

"The question is what happened between 9:20 and 9:45. Here's what I know; Lois Nau said Mike Thompson left Pratt's a few minutes after Mahoney."

He made at tic and labeled it 9:12 then he made another and labeled it 9:22.

"Unless he stopped somewhere, he arrived at Slater Park around that time."

Now he made another tic between 9:45 and 9:55 and labeled it 9:50.

"Police officer Wayne Redenbaugh was making a routine patrol around Lake Okabena that night and pulled into the driveway at Slater Park where he saw Thompson's car with the driver's door open and the keys in the ignition. He looked around a little but didn't find anyone. That's not too unusual because people often get out of their cars and walk around the park or go neck in the bushes. He called base on the radio and reported that he was leaving Slater Park and would check Sunset Park next. His call was logged at 9:52."

I could see where Jim was headed. There was that gap between the 9:22 and 9:45; twenty three minutes.

"Mahoney said no one was at the park when she got there and no one was there when she left. We now have a couple of puzzles. Where was Mike Thompson between 9:22 and 9:45? If Mahoney left at 9:45 and Officer Redenbaugh got there at 9:50 how did Mike Thompson disappear in just five minutes and end up in a sewage pond ten miles away?"

Jim circled the blank interval between 9:22 and 9:45; put the pencil down and looked at me.

"I learned a lot about 'time lines' at the FBI Academy. Once I plotted this out it I could see that there had to be another person involved. Here's what I think happened."

Jim explained his theory. Thompson followed Mahoney to Slater Park he said. Rossberg repeated that Barb denied there was ever anyone at the park while she was there. Someone else must have followed Thompson to the park, met him there and killed him with a blow to the back of his head. But why? Did Thompson attack Mahoney and someone showed up to defend her? Who took the body and dumped it in the sewage pond? Did Mahoney have a new boyfriend? Was he the killer? Rossberg said he checked out the boyfriend angle and he wasn't anywhere near Worthington that day. Jim sat back in his chair and folded his hands behind his head and looked up at the ceiling.

"What do you know that you're not telling me? Was there someone else with Mahoney when she came to the station? Did she tell you anything about what happened at Slater Park?"

"Deputy, I've told you everything I know. Barb and I only talked about our breakup and she was alone. She never even told me she was at Slater Park."

"Does she talk about her new boyfriend? Did he help her?"

I said I didn't know anything about a new boyfriend.

"Is she lying? How do I know that you didn't close the station early and go meet her at the park? Can anyone verify that you were at the station until ten?"

"Arvin Whelan drove in on his motorcycle and bought a couple of bucks worth of gas and was driving away just as Barb drove up. I'm sure he'll remember that."

Rossberg looked down at his time line diagram and shook his head. I'll bet getting me to Slater Park in time to kill Mike Thompson was the only plausible solution he had left. It never occurred to him that Barb could have killed Mike. It never occurred to him that Barbara had Mike's body in her car when she came to see me. It never occurred to him that the shop towel tied me to the sewage pond and connected me to Mike's body. I didn't dare ask him what Barbara had told him; I didn't want to start him down a new path now that he was so lost on the one he was on.

The interview was over and I left the Sheriff's office, went back to the station and finished mounting the tires. The next Tuesday I loaded my car with everything I had and drove to Mankato. I didn't look back.

When I came back for our 60th class reunion, I drove around Worthington looking at familiar landmarks. Pratt's Ice Cream Parlor only lasted a few years but the store front is still the same. Interstate 90 north of town now carries all the tourist traffic so Obie's Standard Station on Oxford Street is long gone. The sewage treatment plant has been expanded along with bigger treatment ponds. Slater Park hasn't changed a bit; even the same old wooden sign is still there. I didn't bring up the Thompson Murder Mystery at the reunion and nobody else did either so I guess it's pretty well forgotten.

As far as I know Barbara never said anything to anyone. When she mentioned her new boyfriend to Rossberg she must have given him an ironclad alibi. So, I'm the only one who knows.

I wonder though. While at the class reunion, I picked up a copy of the Worthington Daily Globe newspaper and took it with me. A few days ago, I was idly leafing through it when a story caught my eye. The city had hired a new female police detective and the article described one of her initial assignments was to review case files on old unsolved serious crimes. The first thought to come to mind was the shop towel I'd dropped at the sewage ponds. If they still have it, would they test it to see if my DNA is on it? I wonder.